A
COLLECTION
OF FIVE
PRIVATE EYE
STORIES

Also by Harry Bryant

# SAINTS OF LOST CAUSES

## HARRY BRYANT

51325 Books

Produced in association with **51325 Books** and Firebird Creative, LLC (Clackamas, OR).

*Always for hire . . .*

First edition: March 2022.

# SAINTS OF LOST CAUSES

# Table of Contents

# INTRODUCTION

I'm going to talk about marketing, which is, frankly, the last thing a writer should talk about, but bear with me for a minute.

Mysteries are different from science fiction, just as they are different from fantasy or romance or horror. All of those genres can have a mystery in them, but if the mystery takes place on the moon, it's a science fiction book. If it has dragons, it's fantasy. If there are tentacled monsters that slurp people's brains out their ears, then it's horror, even if we don't know who the monster is.

It comes to down to bookselling.

I've haunted bookstores all my life. When I was a small lad, the family always took a summer vacation up to Montana (from California), and the best part of the drive was finding new bookstores along the way. At home, Saturday morning family time was a walk to the donut shop and then a visit to the bookstore across the street. I can walk into a bookstore, and just by looking at the shelves, tell you something about the community in which this store is located.

But actual bookselling? Totally different from being a fan of books. Trust me. Bookselling is forgetting what *you* like about books and learning what *everyone* else likes about books. And the most basic thing I've learned and relearned and relearned *again* is that people know what they like, and unless they explicitly ask for something new and different, they want what they want. Your job is to say: "Absolutely!" and "Yes, indeed!" and "Here's another one just like that last one!"

Because reading is entertainment. Reading is comfort food. Reading is curling up with an old friend and being allowed to not be responsible for anything else for a few hours.

True story: Recently, the publisher put a new cover on one of Clive Cussler's older novels. A fellow brought it up to the counter at the bookstore. I recognized him as a regular and pointed out that this book wasn't a "new" Dirk Pitt novel. The customer shrugged. "That's okay," he said. "It's been a while since I read this one. I probably won't remember of it. It might as well be new, you know?"

Anyway, the point here is that sometimes the writer's job is to deliver to expectations. They don't have to invent a new sub-genre. They don't have to re-invent the genre for a new generation. They just have to write to the label on the shelf and tell a good story.

A few years ago, I wrote a book that broke a lot of rules. It was non-linear in its presentation. It was a psychological thriller that never revealed the true identity of the narrator. It ate its own tail several times.

The book I wrote *after* that one was a mystery. Straight-up, no funny business mystery. And I realized I was going to annoy my entire audience if those two books were written by the same author. "Oh, you liked that one? Well, this one is absolutely nothing like that one."

You can't hang a bookseller out to dry like that.

Clearly, I needed a pseudonym.

Which is how Harry Bryant was born. Harry writes mysteries. Harry doesn't sneak supernatural elements into his stories. Harry has no interest in going to the moon. And Harry most certainly does not believe in tentacled monsters that suck people's brains out through their ears. Harry watched a lot of *The Rockford Files* and *Magnum P. I.* in his formative years, and he likes to read John D. MacDonald and Richard Stark. Harry's goal as a writer is to tell stories for readers who like the same things that Harry likes.

Recently, Harry and I chatted about expanding Harry's repertoire. Harry wanted a few more characters to play with. Maybe a new setting. The result of that conversation is this collection.

☆

For The Discrete Detective, we started with a play on the note that Ed McBain always put at the beginning of an 87th Precinct novel.

*While the names of the people and the locations have been changed, everything else in this story is based on actual private investigative procedures and techniques.*

Think of it as a mid-century noir film you've stumbled upon late at night. The city is never named. The characters are archetypes. It probably stars actors you dimly recall from childhood. It rains a lot. Women wear clothing much fancier than anything worn today. No one gets what they want, but what they want doesn't exist anyway . . .

Blake Isaac has been waiting for Harry to write her story for awhile, though the setting came first.

Evergreen is a quaint little town in Eastern Washington state that remains economically viable due to tourism, which it takes very, very seriously. The small town is the quintessential setting for cozies—those mysteries where the stories focus more on the quirky characters who live in the village than the mystery that brings them all into conflict. Sure, it's adorable that everyone has known everyone for several generations, but it's a bit creepy, isn't it? Especially when profit starts to become a factor. Suddenly you realize you may not know your neighbors as well as you thought you did . . .

And speaking of noir, it is typically defined as taking place in an urban setting. I'll quibble a bit (and can cite examples, if you really want to get into the weeds), but fundamentally, noir is about the existential crisis that arises from humanity losing its identity within an environment they have made for themselves. Within these teeming metropolises, it is very easy to feel like you are a widget, an insect, or a nameless drone trapped in a meaningless existence.

Well, Barton Trout used to be one of those poor saps who was defined by the machinery of modern industry. Until he retired. He moved to the coast where the light was better and there were flowering plants and trees. Where he thought he might find himself.

But noir, you know, is more than a setting. It's also a state of mind . . .

All we're going to say about Hecate Hemlock is that, yes, she lives in the Valley. You just take Santa Monica Boulevard to the 101 and then up past Studio City. And yes, the time period is the same as Butch Bliss's. And definitely yes, these two should run into each other . . .

Which bring us to Bliss, who has been Harry's go-to character for these last few years. The Bliss novels start a few years after Butch gets out of prison. We're charting our way to that point in his life when he assumes the mantle of protector of the downtrodden and disadvantaged. But there's a gap between that first day of freedom from prison and the opening of *Hidden Palms*, the first novel. In that gap, he meets a number of characters who become series regulars, and in "Cold Kiss" we get to meet Huggy Bear . . .

Other than Butch, these stories are the first appearance of these characters. You should let Harry know what you think of his new friends. "Hey, Harry, can so-and-so come out and play?"

And Harry will say, "Yeah, I think that could definitely happen."

# AND NOW . . . THE SAINTS

# The
# Discrete Detective

# FETCHING PEACHES

His shadow arrived first, filling the door of my office with a sepulchral gloom. I thought there was an eclipse happening, and cast about for the few things that would be worth saving from my office. Maybe the duck on the file cabinet. Maybe the bottle in the lower right hand drawer. I didn't get much farther than that when he knocked. Solid slab of muscle against the old wooden frame made for a loud report that spooked me out of my list-making.

"Yeah," I said, trying to sound relaxed. "It's open."

The door squealed, trying to rip itself off its hinges and jump out the window. He filled the doorway, and yes, now there was an eclipse.

I kept my hands steady on my desk. "Good afternoon," I said. "What can I do for you?"

He squeezed through the doorway. The top of his head was a finger's width from the ceiling. His shoulders reminded me of a wide-bodied cargo plane, and his hands were the size of highland sheep. An entire herd of cows provided the leather for his jacket, which had been dyed black in memorial of said bovine sacrifice. His cheeks and chin were bare, no hair dared to grow on that craggy surface, and his eyes were like crystalized rocks sunk deep in granite.

"You the investigator?" he rumbled.

"That's what it says on the door," I said.

He looked at the door, read the ornate lettering I had paid a kid ten dollars to do. *Investigations*, it read. *Discrete*, it added.

"Discretion is good," he said. "I got someone to find."

"I've been known to find people."

He crossed to my desk into two steps—it usually took me five or six—and put a small picture on the blotter. Well, it looked small in his hand, but it actually was a pretty good-sized picture. I glanced at it and swallowed hard. "This is a—"

"Can you find her?"

"Her?" I nudged the corner of the picture. It was a professional head shot of a curly-haired poodle. "Yeah, sure. I can find this—this dog."

"Her name is Peaches," he rumbled. "She's very important to me."

"Of course she is," I said. Even though Peaches had a bow in her hair, there was something in her gaze that suggested a darker side. "Tell me about her," I said.

"She's all that matters," he rumbled, and I thought of the sound rocks make as they gather speed coming down a mountainside. "I got a lot of people around me. Telling me who I got to fight. Where I got to go. When I eat; where I sleep; how often I get to shit. That sort of thing, you know."

I didn't, but I nodded like I did.

"I got a fight tomorrow night. At the Forum. Some guy from the Midwest. You hear about this?"

I shook my head. "I've been out of town," I lied.

"Lot of money riding on this game," he said. "Makes folks uptight about things, you know?"

"I do know." We were on more familiar ground here.

"I asked around. You found that Gipperson kid."

"Kid sort of found himself," I said, trying to downplay my involvement. The family matriarch had latched onto a wild idea that I was—somehow—the brains behind the kidnapping and had threatened to set the family firm on me. Mr. Gipperson gave me a little extra to assuage my professional outrage about the slur on my reputation. I took the money and did my best to forget about the family dynamic in that fancy house on the hill. A bottle of rye helped.

Mountain asked a question. "Sorry, what?" I asked.

"Can you find her?" he asked. "Can you find Peaches? By Saturday?"

I glanced at the calendar on the wall. Black 'X's marked off the first few days of the month. This month's curvaceous pinup gave me a supportive wink and a thumbs-up. *You can do this!* proclaimed the banner across the top of the page. "Yeah," I said. "Saturday."

Wasn't a lot of time to dally about.

He reached into his coat and produced a roll of bills that were held together with a gold clip. The clip had a mermaid on it. He thumbed off a couple of bills and put them on my desk. "That enough?" he asked.

It was more than enough. "Sure," I said. I tapped the picture of Peaches. "Can I keep this?" An expression like a storm cloud passed over his face. "I'll give it back," I said. "I just need something to show around."

"Okay," he said. Mountain started to put his money clip away, but then he stopped and pull off one more bill. "But no one can know whose dog it is," he said. "Lot of money riding on this fight. Anyone hears a rumor about a missing dog might start thinking—maybe too much, you know?"

"Right," I said. "Can't have folks thinking you care about something." It came out harder than I meant it, and for a moment, I thought he was going to break my desk. Or me. "Someone," I amended quickly. "Peaches is a not a thing. She's a—she's a real . . ." I trailed off.

"You don't have anyone." He said it matter-of-factly. Not to be rude. Just a simple statement of fact.

I stood up. I wasn't quite tall enough to look him square in the eye, but I gave him a good glimpse of what I had. Of what I knew about the world.

"I don't like guys like you," he said.

"Why is that?"

"You don't stay down." His mouth firmed up. It almost looked like a smile. "But in this instance, she said it was a good thing."

That threw me off my game. "Wait. What?" All the air left me, and I felt like I had been turned to stone.

Mountain squeezed back through the door. "Tomorrow night," he said as he left. "I need my Peaches back by then."

On the desk, the picture of the cute poodle stared at me. Her gaze said she knew how cruel the world was.


I went downstairs to Bushmill's. Sid was working the bar, and he raised an eyebrow when I asked for a cup of coffee. "I'm working," I said.

"This early?" was his response.

I sipped the dark sludge he provided. It punched my tongue, and I considered asking for a shot of whiskey to take the edge off, but swallowed my pride along with the mouthful of coffee.

Someone had left the morning paper on the bar, and I scooped it up. I didn't bother with the front page—same old doom and gloom anyway. Too many people still had night-mares about the war. We weren't bouncing back like they said we would, which was making people wonder why we had elected these bozos. The Metro section had talk about the new construction going on near Cumberland Point, and under the fold, there was an article about a new exhibit at the Metropol-itan Museum. *Prophesies and Portents in Mid-century Art*, or some such nonsense.

Advertising for the shows at the Forum covered the back page of the section. There was a big-top aerialist act tonight, and tomorrow night were the fights. A bunch of mid-weight bouts to get the crowd's blood up, and the big event at nine was a title bout between the Hammer of the Midwest and the reigning champion. The art department had done a good job with a nose-to-nose portrait of the two fighters. A little license with the caricatures, but not too much. The champ really did look like a granite statue. I should know; he had been in my office less than twenty minutes ago.

"You going to this?" I asked Sid.

"The aerialist show? Of course. Wouldn't miss it."

"No." I tapped the champ's face. "The main event."

He wrinkled his nose. "How long have we known each other?" he asked.

"Five—six years, I think," I said.

"Have I ever given you the impression that I'm interested in watching two grown men beat the crap out of each other?"

"I don't think you have," I admitted. I flipped back to the front of the Metro section. "You seen this exhibit?"

"Last week," he said. "It's a little heavy with painters who came out of Mercator's Apocalyptic Tension period, but overall, it's good. You should go."

"I might."

He gave me the eye. "You should take—"

"I might," I stressed.

His mouth worked. "Did I see a celebrity take the back stairs?" His eyes strayed to the paper. "Someone I should recognize?"

I ignored his question. I was discrete, after all. Like it said on the door.

"If I was going to put some money down on this weekend, who would I talk to?" I asked.

He rubbed the side of his head with his thumb. "A little scratch kind of betting or getting yourself in trouble money?" he asked.

"Both. Neither. I'm wondering who the players are these days. It's been a while since I've been to the track."

Sid, like all the barkeeps in town, was tapped into the secret network that ran the city. Sure, there were the mouthpieces who liked to pontificate from the front steps of City Hall, and there were the firebrands who shouted their message from their soapboxes in the Park, but the real machinations played out in dark alleys and well-shadowed back rooms.

"There's Cantrell," Sid said. "Has a table in back of Bloom's. He's the guy you see when you want to get rid of some pocket change. Gurnsey. Tims. Feragano. They've got bigger books, and they're always undercutting each other. Of course, the real action is with the Windsor Twins. They deal with the big fish."

Precisely the sort who would care about someone playing dirty with the champ. If they weren't, in fact, already involved. "They still in Julestown?" I asked nonchalantly. As if I didn't already know.

He nodded. "Yeah. Ivar & Sons."

"Thanks, Sid."

I didn't finish the cup of coffee. Sid wouldn't hold it against me. In fact, he would probably save it under the counter for later, which—come to think of it—was probably why it had tasted so bad. I was drinking yesterday's coffee.

Someone knew Peaches was gone, and it wasn't difficult to surmise that this person was going to make a lot of money when the champ hit the canvas tomorrow night. And if the dog snatcher wasn't the betting sort, then someone near to them was. No bookmaker worth their game would sing about who had placed bets with them, but maybe I could find out who was seeing heavy action. From there, it was a matter of showing up unannounced and asking awkward questions.

My job wasn't that hard: mostly it was about being a wise-ass and trying not to get shot. Some days were better than others.

I started with Cantrell, on the off-chance that this job was going to be easy and I wouldn't have to go uptown.

Bloom's was like Bushmill's, except on the wrong side of the expressway and grimier. The windows weren't clean, and the hanging lights were dingy. Everyone looked sallow and empty-eyed, though, to be fair, what with the recent strike at the rail yard, that was the prevailing mood these days. The place was half-full, a bit of a surprise for mid-morning. Regulars filled most of the stools; you could tell them by the permanent lean to their stools, pushing them closer to the polished bar.

The fancy vinyl booths along the back were roomy enough to seat six, but the Cantrell was the only occupant of his booth. He was a wide man, pudgy of finger and heavy of jowl. Like me, he was a week away from his last shave, but my look was purposefully misanthropic. He was cheap.

Slips covered his table, and he was feverishly working at collating all the pluses and minuses into his ledger.

I decided against dawdling at the bar and pretending to drink. A flat-faced goon with a shaved head and muscles in his neck popped off a chair as I approached Cantrell's booth. I gave him a bored stared. "I'd like to have a word with your boss," I said.

He shook his head.

I pulled a bill from the stack the Mountain had left with me. "How about now?" I asked.

He spat on the floor, letting me know what he thought of my flash, but he plucked the bill from my hand before I put it away. The money disappeared into his pocket and he faded back to his corner chair.

Cantrell had seen our exchange, but he made me wait a minute or two before he looked up. He wore a pair of half-lens glasses and he peered over the top of them. "That's disappointing," he said, referencing his man's price.

I was still holding my wad of cash. "Leaves me more to throw at you," I said.

He snorted. "My book is closed."

I gestured at his slips. "Lot of action you got there."

"I'm doing tax prep," he said. "Gotta make my social contribution and all."

"Sure," I replied. "Kids need hot lunches at schools."

"What do you want?" he snapped.

"What's the spread?"

"I wouldn't know anything about that," he replied. When I started to pocket my roll, his expression changed. "Hang on, sport," he said. "Let's not be too hasty."

I fiddled with the top bill of my roll. "The spread," I said, trying to jog his memory.

"Five to one."

"Really? Folk think the Hammer is going to get hammered that badly?"

His tongue touched his lower lip. "Five to one," he repeated. "In favor of the Hammer."

The mass of paper made sense. I wasn't the only one who thought the spread was wrong. Cantrell wasn't going to disabuse them of their notions. The champ was the champ. There was no way this matchup could be that badly skewed. But it was exactly the kind of pie-in-the-sky betting frenzy that would bring out the crazy. Oh, the greedy ones—the coin-crazed fools—would see that spread as a once-in-a lifetime opportunity.

I pulled a bill free from my wad and dropped it on the table. "What's the story?" I asked. "What's the fable you're spinning when someone comes to drop coin on you?"

"I'm not spinning a thing," Cantrell replied, a hurt look on his face. "I'm telling it true."

I dropped another bill on the table. "So tell it, already."

He reached for my money, and it vanished under his fat fingers. "Hammer's been training," he said.

"They all train," I pointed out.

"This is different," he said. "You remember the snowstorm last winter? The one that put a blanket on the city from Mercury Blvd all the way to docks. Word has it he plowed the streets after the storm passed."

"Plowed the streets?"

"By himself. With an old farm tool."

"That's a little . . . excessive, don't you think?"

"That's dedication," Cantrell said. "That's focus."

"Ah, yes. The sort of focus that makes for a good story," I said. The sort of focus that made you think seriously about the return on a five-to-one bet.

"Thanks, Cantrell," I said.

As I turned to leave, he let out a little whine. "Aren't you—aren't you going to put down some of that stake with me?"

"You said your book was closed."

"I could open it again. For a guy like you."

I tipped my hat at Cantrell's muscle and left without giving the bookie a reply.

I tried the same flex with Gurnsey, but his muscle was better fed and didn't bite. The lights were out at Tim's. I dropped by Feragano's on the off-chance that he had forgotten about our minor disagreement last winter. He hadn't, and I was told to do something unsavory with a shovel and my backside.

I had nothing more substantial than Cantrell's odds of five-to-one. Against the champ. Here I had thought to find one guy or one block of betting that would reveal who knew the champ's weakness. Instead, the money thought the champ was going to break some hearts. All the rubes and the suckers and fools were going for a ride. They couldn't imagine the champ not defending his title.

Was his fall going to happen because of the dog? Was that all it took? Or was there something else in play?

I was out of options downtown. I was going to have to visit the Twins.


A cab was quicker, but I opted for the cable-car instead. It was a more picturesque ride, but I didn't pay attention to the scenery. I had some thinking to do. Not just about the Mountain and his missing dog, but also about how I was going to deal with the uptown crowd. The Twins were going to be difficult to approach, more so because of—well, that was what it was. None of us could change the past. All I could hope for was to convince them that I had something they didn't. That might be enough to get them to overlook other considerations.

I kept patting the side of my jacket, making sure the folded picture was secure in the inner pocket.

Maybe I could tease the Twins into giving something away. Maybe I wouldn't have to beg.

Ivar & Sons was an old family business. The sort of business where everyone—both clients and employees—had been working together for generations. The storefront was a bespoke tailor—suits and hats, mostly, the fancy ball gown, once in a great while. The shop had a dress code, of course. You had to be wearing one of their bespoke suits to get in the door, but since you couldn't get a suit anywhere but there, entry was impossible.

Fortunately, all I needed to do was loiter outside long enough to get someone's attention. It didn't take long.

"You can't stand here, son." He was old enough to be respectful, but the scar tissue around his eyes said he'd have no trouble putting his hands on me when the time came. He wore an Ivar & Sons suit—the line on the trousers was sharp enough to slice a man's throat and the coat was tight enough for me to see his muscles, but not so tight that it restricted his movements.

I had been making eyes at the chocolate brown suit in the display. The suit was so finely tailored that it made the mannequin look smarter than me.

"I'm looking to have a chat with Elsa," I said, name-dropping to let him know I wasn't a gawker.

He shook his head like the name meant nothing to him.

I shrugged like it didn't matter all that much to me. "We'll, I guess I'll try Feragano instead. I'm sure he'll be interested in what I have."

The door guard sucked on a back tooth, wondering if I was bluffing. I nodded at the suit in the window. "Do you have to take the suit off when you go home at night, or do they let you buy on an installment plan?"

He gave me a hard stare. After getting a similar look from the Mountain a few hours ago, this guy's side-eye was like getting grief from a six-year-old when you tell her she can't have any taffy.

When I didn't flinch, he grunted and went into the store.

Through the window, I watched him approach the counter. A woman stood there, and she listened briefly to his report. With a wave of her hand, she sent him back out to deal with me.

"Tell me," he said.

Inside the shop, the woman approached the window. She was sheathed in blue silk, and her hair was pale moonlight wreathed about her head. Her lips were red, and they parted slightly as she stared at me, a hungry familiarity in her eyes.

"I hear the odds for the fight tomorrow night are stretched the wrong way," I said, looking away from her gaze. "The champ's in great shape. I mean, I saw him a few hours ago. Looked like carved granite. Not the sort to go down after a few rounds."

He shrugged. "I don't pay attention to the fights," he said.

"More of a fan of the wire acts?"

His face gave nothing away.

"You probably don't get out much," I guessed. I glanced at the woman again. "There might be a fix. Or not. Hard to say. Be a shame if your boss wasn't . . . well-informed."

He relayed my message, and this time, Elsa's wave was for me.

I went into the shop.


"People have been talking about you," Elsa said over her shoulder as I followed her into the back room of the haberdashery.

"I'm sure they're saying nice things," I said.

The floor was polished wood. Bookcases lined the walls, and well-bound books filled the shelves. A fire slumbered in the fireplace at the end of the room. Displayed on horizontal racks over the mantle were several swords. Not only were they vintage and well-cared for, they were within easy reach.

Elsa strode over to a mahogany side table, where there were several crystal decanters and a full bar set. She poured herself a glass of cloudy alcohol and let me watch her take a sip. It was like watching an icicle melt.

"And if they aren't saying nice things?" she asked.

"Then they're probably true," I admitted. I waited for her to offer me a drink. She didn't.

"I heard that Aurelia Micelene found a missing Van Erkyk recently."

"Did she? I thought she donated one to the Met."

"Ah, yes, of course. My mistake." Elsa gave me a knowing smile. "Talbot said something about the title fight tomorrow night."

"I hear the odds aren't good for the champ."

Her dress shimmered when she raised her shoulders. "Odds are odds," she said. "You don't play the odds."

"No, you play the game. Rather, you make sure you don't get played."

"I'm not sure what you are hinting at."

"Someone is covering that spread. The cynic in me wonders what are the odds on *those* odds. What if someone were playing the rubes and suckers? Getting them wound up about the local hero. Piping them a narrative about an upset. I heard the Hammer regraded all the roads around town—by himself. Did it in an afternoon. That's got to build your endurance. What's the champ been up to recently?"

"I'm sure he's been training. He's very dedicated to his . . . chosen profession."

"Is that what you call it?"

She finished what was in her glass. "Pugilism bores me," she admitted. "Especially of this caliber. All they do is stand there and hit each other."

"You prefer the scrappy sort of knockabout? Maybe something with a little hair pulling and knocking over of the furniture?"

Her cheeks colored slightly at that. I had been too honest, and I regretted it instantly. I should have kept my distance. She turned away as she poured herself another measure. "You should tell me what you know," she said as turned around again. "Before I have Talbot throw you out."

I had been trying to figure out the angle, trying to understand how the spread had gotten to where it was, and how Peaches figured into it. All the gossip was about the Hammer and how prepared he was. No one was talking about the champ. No one was telling stories about his training regime. Which made me wonder about the dog snatching. At first, I thought it had been to get the champ to throw the fight. *Go down in the third round or the dog gets it.* That sort of thing. But now, I wondered if it was the opposite. Take the man's dog so that he was angry. So that he entered the ring in a rage. The sort of rage where you forget to stop.

Five-to-one. What sort of payday would that be for those who sided with the champ?

I got out the picture of Peaches, and I put it on the side table. As she looked at it, I poured myself a finger of booze.

Her face became even more of a mask. "Don't make a mess," she said.

I thought she was admonishing me to be careful with the glassware, but then I realized she was talking to someone behind me. I turned around in time to see Talbot's knuckles as he threw a punch at my face.

*Good catch*, I thought, and then everything went dark.


I heard a dog barking, and at first, I thought it was the furious furball that lived in the apartment next to mine. I went to roll over and bang on the wall, but something held me back. Was I tangled in the sheets of my bed? I couldn't get my arms free. The dog barked more. And then I remembered what happened.

I opened my eyes. My vision swam, and I floated along with it. Gradually, the room came into focus.

I was in a warehouse. Stone floor. Crates of various sizes stacked around me. There was a draft, and the light was cold and brittle. I was tied to a wooden chair. Heavy rope. Good knots. Someone had taken my coat.

I ran my tongue around the inside of my mouth. My lower lip hurt as I stretched it, and my left cheek was sore. I wiggled in the chair and felt a hitch in my side. There was some bruising along my ribs. Talbot had hit me more than once.

The dog had stopped barking. Or maybe there hadn't been a dog, and I had imagined it. I couldn't be sure. The only thing I was sure about was that I was in a pickle.

I bounced up and down in the chair, scraping the wooden legs on the floor. I figured someone would hear me. Eventually, two guys wandered into view. Their suits weren't I & S level bespoke, but their clothes were definitely a step up from what a union box hauler could afford. I dubbed the pair Curly and Shirley. Shirley was the one in charge. "Whatcha doin'?" he asked.

"I was going to ask you the same thing," I said.

Shirley looked at Curly. "Got a mouth on him," he said.

Curly nodded. "Yup." He walked over and smacked me. The punch rang my bell. I waited for the floor to stop spinning.

"See how this works?" Shirley asked.

I checked my lip. The cut from earlier had split again. I tasted blood. "Maybe," I said. "Could you go over it again?"

Curly smacked me once more. This time, I let the blow knock me over. My shoulder took the brunt of the impact against the floor. I managed to not bounce my head. On my side, I wiggled and felt a little play in the ropes.

My hands were tied behind me. Rope looped around my shoulders and my legs. I could stand and move around, but I'd be a turtle with a steamer trunk shoved into his shell.

Shirley grabbed the chair and pulled me upright. He let the chair legs clunk against the floor. He leaned over, putting his mouth close to my ear. "We got all night," he said. "You want to entertain us, go right—"

I snapped my head to the side, slamming the top of my skull into his cheek. He made a noise, and while Curly was standing there, staring at me, I lurched to my feet and charged him. I wasn't fast, but I had the extra weight of the chair with me. I rammed into him and stayed on top as we went down. I bounced in the chair a couple of times, and he made a noise like someone punching a pillow.

I tipped off him, banged my elbow on the floor, and got myself turned around. The ropes around my shoulders were loose, and I got my upper body free. I struggled upright and then collapsed onto Curly's face.

Shirley grabbed my head, his fingers probing for my eyes. I twisted and tried to pull away. The chair got between us, and his grip slipped. I put my feet down and pushed back. I didn't fall over and I kept pushing and pushing. We went backward until we ran into the stacks of crates. Shirley was pinned, and I felt him squirming like a bug. Stumbling, I nearly tripped over the chair leg. I sat down, putting all four legs on the floor and leaned forward, scrabbling at the knots around my ankles. I got them loose, shook my legs free, and stood up.

Now I had a weapon and they didn't. With the odds in my favor, I sent both toughs to slumberland and checked their pockets for useful clues.

Nothing.

I didn't find the dog in the warehouse either. Apparently, I had imagined it.


I was nursing a drink and a bag of ice when she came to the office. If her sister was all ice and angles, she was shadows and curves. Wincing from the bruises on my ribs, I fetched a second glass. I poured her a measure and pushed it across the desk with a knuckle.

"I warned her," Ilsa said. She was wearing a fur coat that covered her from her chin to knee. When she crossed her legs, the coat rippled around her like a living thing, and I glimpsed silvered stockings. She was wearing scarlet pumps. They matched the rubies dripping from her ears.

I shifted the bag of ice against my back. "You mentioned me to the Mountain too, didn't you?"

"The Mountain?"

I gave her a look that said I knew she knew who I was talking about, and she inclined her head a fraction.

"Where's the dog?" I asked.

"That's the wrong question," she said. "You should ask: who gave him the dog in the first place?"

But I knew the answer to that question. What I didn't know was which way the fight was supposed to go. Had Elsa swiped Peaches to put the champ off his game? Or was the loss of his favorite friend supposed to put him in a mean mood? But now that I had Ilsa Windsor in my office, classing up the place, I wondered if I was missing the larger game.

This wasn't about the fights. It was about family.

Ilsa had sent the champ to see me, knowing that if the dog came back, it would upend whatever scheme her sister was running. But if I did, it would put another black mark next to my name in Elsa's ledger. How many marks could a man have before she drew a line through his name?

Ilsa, sensing my thoughts, raised her glass. "Tough choice," she said.

"No choice at all, really," I said.

"I know," she replied. She drank the whiskey and put the glass on my desk. She stood and ran her hands along her coat, soothing it. I thought about what she was wearing underneath the coat.

When she looked at me, I knew she saw those thoughts on my face. She smiled. "Are you going to come by tonight?"

"Probably," I said. "It won't be any easier tomorrow."

She nodded. "I'll leave the garden gate unlocked."

After she left, I dug out the crumpled picture of Peaches I had found in Shirley's jacket pocket. I spread it out on the desk, and the dog stared at me. A hint of a smile. If you believed dogs could smile.

The picture curled when I let go of it. I grabbed Ilsa's glass and used it to hold the picture down. I poured myself a drink and splashed a bit in her glass for good measure.

Her lipstick was stark against the rim.

"Yeah," I said to the empty room. "It's good to have someone."

I finished my drink, put on my coat, and went to fetch Peaches.

✳

Blake Isaacs

Black Eye Investigations

# CHASING BIGFOOT

On the third night of her stake-out, Blake Isaacs spotted Bigfoot.

Sasquatch sightings in the national forest around Evergreen were ubiquitous enough to warrant their own section in McGarrity's Shirtopia—the tourist shop of tourist shops at the south end of Main. The display was four t-shirts wide and it went up to the ceiling. Everything from "Squatch it!" To "I Saw the Big Dude and all I have to prove it is this stupid t-shirt" to "Hug your squatch," and every design came in fourteen colors. Every resident of Washington State's most self-aware tourist destination had a Bigfoot story, and many of these stories had been told so often that anyone sitting at the bar in The Olde Canard could finish the story while you paused to wet your throat.

Not that Blake thought the figure she glimpsed through the trees was actually the elusive cryptid. There was a perfectly rational explanation for who was in the woods that night. But, for a moment, as she heard it—no, it wasn't an "it"—as she heard *whoever* it was, she couldn't help herself. *Wait 'til I tell the gang!*

She was sitting with her back against an old pine, a folded up tarp beneath her to keep from getting wet. She was wearing the dark lining of her winter coat—the coat being a shade at the opposite end of the *How to be Invisible in the Woods* palette—a pair of fleece leggings over her warmest tights, and a scarf knitted by one of the Mother Hens. With one earbud, she had been listening to a history podcast, hoping it would keep her awake. She might have nodded off. It had been awhile since she had dared to check her phone, and the two guys mumbling in her ear weren't talking about Nero's rule of Rome anymore. However, when she heard the heavy whisper of tree branches being brushed aside, her drowsiness vanished.

The moon was a partial sliver, and clouds kept darting in front of it. She yanked out her earbud as she peered into the deep shadows among the trees. Yes, there it was. The sound of something large moving through the forest.

Part of her brain couldn't stop imagining a large, hairy creature with enormous feet and a heavy occipital forehead ridge.

*It's not Bigfoot*, she chided herself. More likely, it was the reason she was out here, practicing her meditative breathing and trying not to freeze her ass off. The nights were getting cold already. The warm air that rolled in from the Pacific was slow and heavy with rain, but by the time it rolled over the Cascades, it had dumped a lot of that weight. All that remained was a whisper of sleet and a petulant bite. Local farmers felt that bite. Many had taken their harvests already, and there was talk about a hard winter.

All of which had been part of the conversation Derek Hunter had had with her a few days ago. *Someone is stealing from me,* he had said. *I don't know exactly what or how, but my bills are up and my sales are down.*

Derek ran Grassbow Orchards, a boutique operation that produced a Honeycrisp apple that was a tremendous hit in the Seattle market. The hot summer and abruptly cool fall had confused his trees. The apples had ripened fast and spoiled faster. His season was already over, and yet, his water and electrical consumption was still at the same level of late spring. Additionally, materials—tubing, plastic sheeting, fertilizer— were disappearing from his storehouse.

*Maybe you've got a break in a water line somewhere,* Blake had suggested, *or a pump is malfunctioning.*

*The irrigation system is all above-ground,* Derek said. *We roll it up in the winter.*

And without a better explanation, Blake had said she'd look into it, which is how she came to be spending her nights in the woods, shivering under an ancient pine near the north corner of the property, listening to podcasts, and trying to stay warm.

Light flickered in the trees. A flashlight swept back and forth. It hesitated, illuminating a spot on the ground, and then it jiggled. The beam turned up, shining into the trees, and then it clicked off.

Blake, focused on the woods like a hunting dog pointing toward game, heard a sound like a log falling, and a few seconds later, heard it again. *How often do two trees fall in the forest?* she thought.

The light clicked on, and then off again. The swishing sound started once more, and she got the sense that whatever— *whoever*, she reminded herself—was moving away.

She crept through the forest, taking her time. Trying not to make any noise. Distances were hard to judge in the pallid moonlight, but when she felt like she had reached the spot where *whoever* had been, she fumbled in her pocket for her red-lensed flashlight. Cupping her hand around the narrow device, she clicked it on.

A yard or two ahead of her, there was a shallow impression in the ground. A little ragged, but it was clearly a footprint. A very large footprint.

"Okay, okay. You got me." Holly Valance laughed.

"No, I'm serious," Blake said. "It was a giant footprint."

Holly shook her head as she tapped the metal pitcher of steamed milk against the counter. "My dad was the worst for these sorts of stories. You remember that time he had us convinced that there was a baby 'squatch living in the gully behind the house?"

Blake drummed her fingers on the counter. "Was that the summer the mountain lion killed Mrs. Perkins's dog?"

"No, that was a couple years later. This was the year that Billy Cartwright kept coming by my house."

"Oh, right. And your dad was trying to keep you from sneaking out at night . . ."

The espresso machine finished gurgling, and Holly poured the two extra-large shots into the tall paper cup. Blake eyed it with the feral fascination of the sleep-deprived. Holly laid a spoon across the top of the steamed milk and poured. Blake tried not to fidget as Holly doodled in the foam, drawing a swirly swirl that swirled back on itself.

"No, seriously." Holly put a lid on the cup and placed it on the counter in front of Blake. "What did you see up there?"

Blake grabbed the cup, took a large sip, and scalded her tongue. "I am serious," she said. She unlocked her phone and showed Holly the pictures she had taken. Holly unconsciously tucked a strand of blonde hair behind her ear as she leaned forward.

Anyone peering in through the front window of Grounds for Life—the adorable coffee shop right across the green from the statue of Gaston de Scheldt, the Belgian rail magnate who built the first home in Evergreen—would think they were sisters, but they weren't. They had grown up on the same street, gone to the same schools, and dated the same boys (but not at the same time). Everyone thought they would go to the same fancy college back east, but something happened their senior year. Holly left Evergreen—"fled" is how some people spoke of her departure—and went to school in New York City or Boston or someplace like that. Blake stayed in the Pacific Northwest. Studied criminology at the U of W. Joined the Seattle Police Department after graduation. Did her time in uniform. Was on track to make Detective before she was thirty—oh, her dad would have been so proud—but, well, her life took a hard turn.

Blake came back to Evergreen, crawled to into her old bedroom where she intended to stay—forever, as far as she cared. Her mother was happy to see her baby girl again. She didn't care about the nonsense reported in *The Seattle Times* about Blake. What mother would? However, she drew the line at "forever." *You can't keep doing this,* she had said to Blake one day.

*Why not?* Blake had countered, hating the sulky tone that came out of her mouth but was too tired and too hurt to reach for something else.

*For one, the bed is too short,* her mother said.

*I'll sleep on the floor,* Blake replied.

Her mother gave her the Look—that side-eye every mother has when their children insist on being an immovable object in a perpetually accelerating world—and Blake, escaping the withering heat of that look, threw on sweatpants and a hoodie and took her sulk elsewhere. Without thinking about where she was going, she ended up at the coffee shop, because Grounds for Life—it had been called Coffee Central back when she was in high school—was always where they ended up. And that was when she met the new owner who had been Holly Waggoner while she had been away from Evergreen, but who was now Holly Valance once again.

They didn't make eye contact that first day, and when Blake returned later in the week, they eyed one another warily, assessing the thickness of the hoary ice between them. Neither remembers who made the first attempt to breach that wall, but an attempt was made. They weren't besties—both were too cynical and too armored for that sort of hashtag foolishness— but they recognized a level of connectedness between them, and maybe that was enough.

"Well, okay, that certainly looks like a footprint," Holly said, looking at the shiny pictures Blake had taken. After creeping around in the dark for another hour, Blake had found no other evidence that someone was out there, and it had taken her another hour of scouring the woods to find the footprints again. By that time, she was well past tired. Her *Give a Shit* meter was in the red. She had flicked on the flash, took a couple pictures, and gone home.

In the morning, the series of black-on-black with shiny bit of black were a sorry summary of the night's efforts.

"What are you going to tell Derek?" Holly asked.

"I can't tell him Bigfoot is stealing his water," Blake said. "I might as well go beg Mig for a job hustling tees at the booth. Or heck, since I'm a big girl now, maybe I can be a manager and do a special project."

Working the Shirtopia summer tourist booth was a rite of passage for high school students at Evergreen High. Roger McGarrity—who was savvier than sleazy, but only by a narrow margin—had a long-standing arrangement with the local school district wherein summer "internships" at his t-shirt booth translated to approved credits in a variety of categories: Economics, Sociology, Washington State History, Speech and Debate. McGarrity graded on a very simple criteria: how many shirts did you sell during a season? And not for nothing did the fit of a classic Sasquatch-sighting t-shirt matter.

Holly wrinkled her nose. "Isn't it late in the year for foot-printing?"

"I don't know," Blake sighed. She took another sip of her coffee. It was still too hot, and the caffeine still hadn't hit her system. It was going to be a long day.


Blake's office was on the top floor of the Keystroke Building, and it was a long and narrow room with sloped ceilings. Like all the buildings along Guilder Lane, the Keystroke was part of the Flemish architecture remodeling championed by the LIIEC—the Lifestyle Improvement in Evergreen Council— and it proudly displayed the classic stepped gable. From her large window, Blake could see the statue of Gaston de Scheldt, the ornate facade of the Hanseatic Hotel, and a bit of the garish window display of Shirtopia. She could also see into the window of the top-floor office of the building across the lane. Fortunately, the blinds were rarely open.

This was where she ran Black Eye Investigations, her solution to her mother's side-eye about getting out of the house after her spectacular fall from grace at the SPD. She was halfway through a three-year lease on the space, and it was still entirely up in the air whether she would default on the lease before it ran out.

She was the only licensed private investigator in Evergreen, one of six in all of Cascade County, and most of her client communications were a single line that she copy-and-pasted in her summary emails. "No data to report for the background check." Two billable hours, max.

A surveillance gig, while boring in an entirely different way, meant a lot more billable hours. She couldn't fuck this up. She needed something that resembled an actual case.

While her computer booted up, she stood at the window and watched the tourists gaggle about along the pedestrians-only road. It was early in the week, and the remnants of last weekend's festival were being replaced with shiny signage for this weekend's festival. LIIEC proudly boasted that Evergreen had the most specialty festivals of any tourist destination on the West Coast. The residents of Evergreen liked to complain there were more festivals than weekends in a year—a factoid which Victor Wannamaker, the chair of the LIIEC, was always eager to correct. *There isn't an event during the last weekend in February,* he would remind people.

Unless it was a leap year. That was when the Intercalary Historical Society held their quadrennial "Leapers" festival. Everyone dressed up like Mark Twain and gathered at Twin Pines Park for an evening of open mic monologues.

Anyway, when her computer was ready, Blake transferred the pictures from her phone. She opened them up on her big monitor, and after tweaking the contrast *a lot*, she could identify what she had seen out in the forest: an oversized, somewhat human-looking footprint.

She had found two footprints, a number which matched the tree-falling noises she had heard. Even in her caffeine-deprived state, Blake could connect those dots. What she had heard was someone using an imprinter—almost like a giant rubber stamp—to make those tracks. The question was: *Why?*

Blake checked her email, surfed the Internet, put her feet on her desk and stared at the ceiling, and finished her coffee. No better idea came to her during that time.

She was going to have to talk to McGarrity.

In another time, Roger McGarrity would have been the master of ceremonies for a traveling circus. It was all flash and show with him, but for all his bluster, he was more fat than florid, more garrulous than loquacious, and more miserly than penny-pinching. However, you couldn't overlook that Mig— as everyone who had ever worked the Shirtopia summer booth called him—was, in many ways, the cornerstone to the economic revival of Evergreen. He had been responsible for the creation of LIIEC; he had drafted the initial proposal that turned the economically depressed town into a tourist desti- nation; and, in his mind, the revitalization of the town pivoted around his store: Shirtopia—the best and most extensive collection of unique t-shirt designs in all of North America.

All of which were printed in China, but that was a reflection of Mig's business acumen and not a revelation of some under- lying hypocrisy.

Once upon a time, a student doing the summer internship at the t-shirt booth had filed a harassment claim against Mig, citing an unreasonable workplace environment. Mig, this student claimed, did not stare at his chest and did not ask him to model new t-shirt designs, which he felt was clearly sexist and discriminatory. Many of this student's peers rolled their eyes and wondered if the kid was trying for some sort of performance art credit. Mig wandered around like a wounded bear for weeks, and the desultory mood made for one of the longest summers anyone could remember.

The student graduated with honors, went off to a prestigious school somewhere, and probably became a lawyer. For a year or two, incoming interns tried to remind Mig of the lesson that the lawsuit had attempted, but it was like trying to dam the Columbia River with a box of toothpicks. Like the relentless flow of the river, things went back to the way they were.

There was a young man working the counter at Shirtopia when Blake entered. He was gawky and spindly, and for a moment, Blake felt very old. Surely she had never looked *that* scrawny and awkward, but in the back of her head, a tiny voice said *Oh, honey* in a decidedly Mother Hen tone.

"Hello, and welcome to Shirtopia, the world's largest emporium of—"

"Is Mig around?" she asked, interrupting the kid's spiel.

"Uh, who—oh! Mr. McGarrity? I, uh, yeah. He's—" The kid stopped. He adopted a stiffer position and tried to deepen his voice. "Mr. McGarrity is in a meeting. Is there something I can do for you?"

Blake sighed. *Sometimes you have to rip the band-aid off,* she thought. "Yeah, can tell him that Hot Tits Ninety-Six wants to have a chat?"

The kid's eyes went exactly where she thought they would go. He blushed when he realized what he had done, and he practically scurried through the hanging curtain to the back portion of the shop.

Of course, there were times when *The Way Things Were* was actually helpful.

The hanging curtain puffed out as McGarrity made his entrance. "Hello, hello, hello," he boomed, projecting his voice like he was working the back row of seats at Sunset Pavilion. He wore a purple t-shirt that proclaimed some nonsense about the meta recursiveness of memes, a pair of baggy plaid shorts, and white socks with Birkenstock sandals.

Blake hated that fashion. Wasn't the whole point of sandals that you didn't have to wear socks?

Anyway, she kept her expression civil and did her best to smile as McGarrity's gaze locked onto her chest.

"It's been a few years, hasn't it? Look at you. All grown up."

And now, she regretted having reminded Mig of her summer internship—even though it had been the quickest way to get his attention—because all she wanted to do was punch him in the throat. In a flash, she was back at SPD training, those first few weeks when everyone was swinging their dicks and puffing out their chests. It wasn't a flight instinct that was putting a torch to everything in the back of her mind; it was a clear-eyed, red-raged instinct to fight back. That same instinct which had gotten her several reprimands and a series of cautionary chats with her watch commander.

Blake offered him one of her business cards, and he stared at it for a long time, as if he wasn't sure what it said.

It read "Black Eye Investigations" across the top, listed her name and contact info, and finished with the pithy catch-phrase the marketing guru had suggested: "We're in your corner." She wasn't sure she had gotten her money's worth, but she was going to use the cards until she ran out, and she had nine hundred and forty-some-odd to go.

"Blake," Mig muttered. "Blake, Blake, Blake." He snapped his fingers. "Yes, yes. Ninety-six. Yes, of course."

Blake kept her smile locked in place while Mig worked through his labyrinthine memory. She had actually worked the booth in '95, but "Hot Tits Ninety-Five" didn't have the same ring to it, and she doubted he was going to check his employment records.

*If he has an actual scrapbook, so help me God . . .* Blake shoved that thought aside as she launched into her story.

"You know? I was talking with a friend of mine, and we were reminiscing about all those Bigfoot sightings back in the day. You remember them, don't you?"

Of course he did. Just look at the 'Squatch wall over there.

"Well, I remember Jimmy Doogan talking about a special

project he had. Him and Freddy Lowenstein. They wouldn't tell us exactly what it was, but they said they got paid extra." Blake cocked her head. "Is any of this ringing a bell?"

Mig shook his head slowly. "No, nope, no," he mumbled.

Blake unlocked her phone and swiped to the pictures she had taken last night. "Something like this," she said, showing Mig the picture of the footprint. "They said they made all those footprints people were talking about, down by Iceflow Creek. Said you gave them cash."

Mig frowned and squinted. "Jimmy Doogan . . . I don't— you know, I don't recall every employee I had, especially those from, I dunno, so long ago."

*It wasn't that long ago, you jackass*, Blake thought. "No? Huh. Well, I guess I can go find Jimmy Doogan. He probably still lives around here. Maybe he'll remember." She made a show of looking at the photo on her phone and then showing it to Mig again. "Heck, maybe he's the one who made this. Wouldn't that be something?"

Mig forced a grin onto his face; it was the sort of expression you see on a carny's face when you're hemming and hawing about opening your wallet for another chance at the dart toss.

Blake let her smile slip. A crack opened in her gaze, and she let him have a peek inside her head. He flinched a little, which was enough.

*You've got to understand the source of that temper*, the SPD-directed therapist had told her. *Until you do, it will hold you back.*

*It's what keeps me going*, she had said.

Her therapist hadn't bothered to ask how that working for her. They both knew.

Twenty minutes later, McGarrity hurried out of Shirtopia. He puffed his way to the lot at the end of the block and climbed into a dingy gray Mazda. When he left the lot and turned north on Decklan Avenue, Blake nosed out of her curbside parking spot and fell in behind him. He drove out to Highway 11 and turned down Holgate Road.

Blake hung back a little. There wasn't much out Holgate except farms and fields. If he turned off, she'd spot him.

However, he didn't go very far. There was older self-storage place about a mile from the interchange. She drove past as McGarrity was waiting for the security gate to open. Turning around at the next driveway, she found a spot nearby where she could pull her car far enough off the road to not be a nuisance. She grabbed her thermal liner from the back of the car, along with her SLR camera bag. The one with the telephoto lens.

There was an inch of water in the ditch alongside the road. She tried not to think about her shoes as she squelched across the ditch and scrambled up the other side.

She didn't see McGarrity's car, and in order to get closer, Blake climbed over a barbed wire fence and cut across a pasture. The grass was uneven and the ground was bumpy—cattle hadn't grazed here for awhile, and moles and ground hogs had taken over. She found a natural dip where she could hunker down and make less of a spectacle of herself. She got her camera out. It already had the mid-range lens on it, and she quickly focused on the gray Mazda.

The car was parked next to a series of roll-up units. McGarrity hadn't turned on an interior light, so she couldn't see much of what was inside the unit that was open. If she wanted to see more, she was going to have to get a lot closer. Like "inside the fence and leaning across the hood of the Maza" sort of closer. She settled for taking a picture of the unit number.

"Why did you come running out here, Mig?" she wondered out loud.

It was possible that his sudden need to do digging around a storage unit had nothing to do with her visit, but she thought it unlikely. The ground was damp and her shoes were wet. She hadn't planned well, and she hoped he wasn't going to be there long. *Come on*, she thought. *Find what you're looking for.*

He did. Or, rather, he didn't. When he came out of the unit, his hands were empty. Blake took a bunch of pictures as he closed up the unit and got back into his car. When she looked at the pictures later, she confirmed her suspicion: Mig was not happy. Something was missing.

By the time she got back to her vehicle, however, he had left the storage facility. When she reached the Highway 11 interchange, she had no idea where he had gone.

"That's kind of embarrassing," Holly pointed out the following morning as Blake brought her up to speed. "I mean, you're supposed to be good at following people."

"It's not all about following people," Blake said. "There are other things to do too."

"Oh, okay. Like what? What else did you find out?"

Blake hesitated. "Well . . . not much, actually."

"Not much?"

"Nothing really concrete. Just . . ."

"Suspicious noises? Did you hear owls hooting or something?"

"No, no. I went home, took a nap so that I could stay up all night and hang out in the woods again."

"It sounds like so much fun. Did you see Bigfoot?"

"I didn't see anything."

"I liked this story better yesterday when you were trying to pretend you *had* seen Bigfoot." Holly nodded at a customer who was looking at the pastry case.

Blake sat and sipped her coffee. She hadn't seen anything during her nocturnal watch, but that didn't mean the night had been a bust. Several times, she had felt like she wasn't alone out there. She had found a spot closer to the outbuildings, and every hour or so, she had done a loose patrol around the property. The place was quiet, except for the somnambulant churn of idle machinery, but she hadn't been able to shake an itch between her shoulder blades.

The footprints were gone. She had searched the woods, but eventually, she had to admit that someone had come through and scuffed up the terrain. Who? Why? When? Lots of questions. The one thing she was sure about was that the only people who knew she had found the footprints were Holly and McGarrity. Oh, and the kid who had been working in Shirtopia when she had stopped by. And the person who made the footprints. *Was that it? Yes, that was it. Five people.*

*Well, four.* She could take Holly off the list for obvious reasons. Probably drop the kid too. That left three, well, two. She didn't need to count herself. That left McGarrity and the person who had made the footprints. She didn't have to squint too hard to imagine a connection between McGarrity and the footprint-maker.

But why? How?

"Crack the case yet?" Holly asked when she returned.

"No," Blake groused.

And the bigger question: what did any of this have to do with the missing supplies and utilities at Grassbow Orchard?

"You should talk to a professional," Holly offered.

"I am a professional," Blake snapped.

"No, I mean a professional cryptozoologist or something."

"That's a thing?"

"Well, I don't know if you can get an accredited degree in it, but doesn't Lucy at the Historical Society have a son or a nephew who is into conspiracy theories and UFOs?"

"Oh, that's just what I need."

Holly gave her a look that said *No, what you really need is someone to take some of that stress out of your shoulders, if you know what I mean.*

Blake sighed. She was overdue to drive over to Seattle for a therapy session. *Maybe this weekend*, she thought. There had to be a group she could visit. "Yeah, okay," she said. "I'll go talk to Lucy."

☆

Instead of walking across the square to the Evergreen Historical Society, Blake drove out to Grassbow Orchards. She thought
that looking at the spot in the woods in the daylight might be
helpful. It wasn't. Daylight only made it more clear there was
no evidence to back up her pictures. The footprints were gone.

She was in a sour mood as she wandered out of the woods.
She skirted the north orchard and cut through the gap between
the barn and the processing shed. The only person she saw was
a younger man unloading a trailer of boxes into the barn. He
stared at her as she walked past. "Hello? Can I help you?"

"Oh, sorry," she said. "I'm here to see Derek."

"He's in the showroom," the guy said.

"Yeah, I know," Blake said. "I was just . . ."

"Just what?"

Blake cocked her head and looked at the man. Same sort of curly
brown hair as Derek. Same shape of face. But this guy couldn't
grow a beard as readily as Derek. All he had was a narrow goatee
that looked like someone had glued it on. "You're—" She tried to
remember the info she had read about Grassbow when she had
taken the job. "You're Daniel," she said. "Derek's brother."

A look of suspicion passed over his face. "Who are you?"

"I'm Blake. Blake Issacs. Black Eye Investigations." She
offered him a card, which he took reluctantly. *Nine hundred
and forty-four to go!*

"An investigator?"

"Yeah, didn't he tell you?"

"Tell me what?"

Blake held her tongue, her thoughts all jumbled in her head.
"Derek's in the showroom?" She jerked her thumb toward the
main building.

"Yeah," the guy said. He looked at her card again and frowned.
"What are you doing here?" he asked. His look of suspicion
deepened.

"Ask your brother," Blake said as she fled.

She had a minute or two head start.

When Daniel burst into the Derek's office, she was sitting on the couch like she had been there for an hour. Derek looked at his younger brother in that way all elder children did when, as children, they were told they had to share with their sibling. "What?" he asked.

"I was—she's—" Daniel waved Blake's card. "She was trespassing."

"I hired her," Derek said. "She's not trespassing."

"Why—why'd you hire her?"

"I'm losing money. Why else would you hire a private investigator?"

"How . . . how are you—we—how are we losing money?"

I noticed how he had inserted himself into the conversation.

"*I*—" Derek said, stressing the power structure within the company. "I have noticed some discrepancies, and I wanted to get a second opinion."

"You couldn't ask me?" Daniel tried not to whine and pout, and failed on both counts.

"You haven't been around that much."

"I've been here all week," Daniel said. "Last week too. I've been putting in some hours, man."

"That's not what I mean," Derek said.

Daniel stiffened. "What do you mean?"

"Look—" Derek sighed. "Look, Daniel. The harvest sucked this year. We're going to have to—well, I don't what we're going to have to do, but we're going to have to do something. The bank is going to want payments. I'm not sure we're going to make it to next season. Not without having to . . ."

"Having to what?"

"I don't know, Daniel. I don't know."

Daniel flung an arm at Blake. "So why are you hiring a PI? How is that helping?"

"Someone is stealing from us," Derek said.

"Stealing? What do you mean?"

"I mean, supplies are going missing. The water bill is up. Really up. So is electricity. But we're already done with this season's crop. There's no reason for this kind of expense. And if there's a leak . . . " He spread his hands. "We're going to have to bring in someone to find it. Who knows how long that'll take. Or how much it'll cost to repair."

"What—" Daniel had gone pale. "What—" He tried again. Got one word out and stopped. He swallowed heavily. "What if there's something . . ."

"What kind of something?" Derek asked.

Daniel's face hardened. "Nothing," he said. "I don't know. I wasn't—" He half-turned toward the door. "I gotta finish unloading that gear," he said. He left without another word, leaving Derek and Blake to stare at one another.

"Okay, you two have an interesting family dynamic," Blake said eventually.

Derek frowned. "I'm not sure what that was all about," he admitted.

"I do," Blake said. "Your brother has a naughty secret he doesn't want to tell you." And when Derek didn't protest, she nodded. "You knew, didn't you? That's why you hired me and didn't tell him. If someone else caught him, then it wasn't you being his big brother, all up in his business."

Derek stared at the wood grain of his desk. "He's always been a bit of a flake, honestly," he said. "It's the family business, but someone has to actually run the company. Take care of the books. Work the distribution channel. I had been doing it for years with Dad, while Daniel . . . Daniel was busy being . . ."

"A fuckup?"

"Daniel," Derek said. "He was busy being Daniel."

"Sure, okay."

"After Dad died, whatever job Daniel had—whatever business scheme he was doing—it all fell apart. It wasn't the first time, frankly. Dad had bailed him out before, and I think he expected I would write a check, just like Dad had. But I couldn't. Everything was tied up in the business. I couldn't give Daniel a bunch of money and pretend I didn't know where it had come from. What was I going to tell the accountant?"

"So you had to give him a real job instead."

"Yeah. I gave him a fancy title: Marketing Director in Charge of Product Placement in New Media Opportunities."

"What is that?" Blake asked. "Talking celebrities into being photographed eating your apples?"

"Basically," Derek said. "He had a small expense account, and I didn't ask what he was doing. And most of the time, it was fine. But we had that hot summer last year and the winter was weird, and this past season was—"

Blake nodded. There had been less snow last year, and the freeze came late and stayed longer. Forest fires over the summer had blanketed the valley with acrid smoke for weeks. Several wineries didn't even bother bottling their grapes; they knew the wine was going to turn out ashy and dry.

"I have a question," Blake said.

Derek raised his head. "Yeah?"

"Did your brother ever work for McGarrity? Shirtopia. The summer intern program."

"The t-shirt guy?" Derek nodded. "I think so." A smile tugged at his mouth. "We all did, didn't we?"

"I suppose so. How'd Daniel do? Is he a good salesperson? Creative thinker? Outside the box sort of fellow?"

"Yeah, maybe. Sure. I guess that's a good way to think about."

"What do you mean?"

"My father raised us to work hard. Get the job done, you know? Ax to the grindstone. Boots on the ground. That sort of attitude, right?"

Blake nodded. It had been the same with her father. It was a generational thing.

"And Daniel could do it, but he preferred not to. He had other things he wanted to do, and school work and work on the farm all got in the way. He worked really hard at figuring out how not to work."

"Ah," Blake said. "Outside the box."

"Yeah, outside the box."

"I bet McGarrity loved him."

Derek didn't follow her train of thought. "What do you mean?"

"McGarrity had . . . let's call them 'extra credit projects' for outside the box thinkers."

Derek's face darkened. "Drugs," he said.

"No, I was talking about—" Blake stopped. "Wait. What?"

"Drugs. Isn't that what you're talking about?"

"No, I was talking about fabricating Sasquatch sightings to drive up tourist activity."

"He did that?"

"He didn't, but he had some kids do it for him." Blake waved her hand. "What drugs are you talking about?"

Derek looked at her. "Weed," he said. His stare got more intense. "Didn't you . . . ?"

"I got a degree in criminology and joined the Seattle Police Department," Blake said. "I certainly did not smoke weed in high school."

"But you knew people who did."

"Of course. I wasn't a total prude."

Derek laughed.

"What?"

Derek leaned back in his chair and gave her a knowing look. "I remember you, you know."

"Remember me?"

"Yeah. You were a year ahead of me. In school."

Blake flushed, recalling what she had said that had prompted him to laugh. "Anyway," she said when she got herself together. "Are you saying that Mig sold pot?"

"I—yeah. Yeah, he did. Well, that was the rumor. I never bought any, but I knew some kids who always had it and—"

"Including your brother?"

Derek hesitated. "Yeah, including my brother."

"Do you think he was dealing?"

Derek thought for a moment. "I don't know," he said. "Maybe." He scratched a fingernail across his desk, chasing some groove he had worn over the years.

Blake could tell he was thinking about something, and she had an idea what it was. In her head, working from a different direction—Shirtopia special projects, 'squatch footprints, what boys do in the woods when they are bored—she had reached the same conclusion. "He's got a grow operation, doesn't he?"

Derek's shoulders slumped. "Jesus," he said. "It makes sense, doesn't it?"

Blake cleared her throat. "I mean, I could keep looking if you—"

"No, no. That's fine. You don't need to. I'll—I'll take care of it."

"You sure?"

"Yeah, I'm sure." Derek tapped his fingers on the desk. "There's no need to, you know . . ."

"Yeah, sure," Blake said, not sure at all. "So . . . we're done, then?"

Derek came back from wherever his thoughts had taken him. "Yeah, yeah," he said quickly. "That'll be it. Thanks."

"Should I bill you . . . ?"

Derek nodded quickly. "Yeah. Go ahead and bill me."

"I'll just—" Blake stood and indicated the door. "I'll get that bill in the mail," she said.

Blake walked back to her car and sat for awhile, a little confused as to what had happened. On the one hand, she had billable hours, and oh yes, she was going to charge him extra for the night time survelliance. On the other hand . . .

She looked out at the rows of apple trees. *Can you blame him?* she thought. The harvest had sucked. The farm was in trouble. Why shouldn't they think about alternative crops?

She could see the look on Holly's face. *Wait. They're growing what?*

No, she couldn't tell Holly. Not any of the details. *Just a bunch of kids goofing off in the woods.* That's what she'd tell her. *Faking footprints. Like we used to do. Chasing things that weren't there.*

As she drove down the hill, Blake had a realization. *Maybe it's time,* she thought. *Maybe it's time we all stopped chasing things that weren't here.*

For the first time in a long time, Blake Isaacs's thoughts turned to the future, instead of the past.

*I'm definitely padding my bill,* she thought.

᠅

# Barton Trout

# THE FINISHER

Dahlia found him in his usual spot, working on a seascape. It was mostly blues and grays—very true to the season—but his brush was building tension in the clouds. A craggy rock in the foreground was being beaten by a wave. Dahlia liked the rock. It looked strong and resolute. Like it wasn't going to take any shit from the sea.

"Watch your language," Trout said when she told him what she thought.

"My dad says worse," she replied.

His brush paused. He turned his head and looked at her. Saw the ball cap pulled low. Saw how she instinctively ducked her head. Noticed the color of her cheeks. That she wasn't wearing a coat. She had ridden her bike out to the scenic turnout at the end of the bluff.

"Everything okay?" he asked.

"It's fine," she said.

Trout dipped his brush in water, wiped it on his rag, and swiped it through the blues on his working board. "All right," he said.

She dug into the pockets of her jean shorts and pulled out a handful of crumpled paper. It took him a second to realize it was money. "I want to hire you," she said.

"What for?" he asked.

She raised her head, and he looked at the blues and purples mottling the skin around her eye. Her lip was puffy.

"I'm sorry," Trout said. "I don't—I don't do that sort of thing," he added.

Eventually, she left, and he listened to the creak of her bicycle wheel until the sound vanished beneath the persistent rush of the waves against the rocks at the base of the cliff.

She had smoothed out the bills and placed them under a rock so they wouldn't blow away. With a sigh, he bent, favoring his leg, and retrieved the money. Mixed bills. Mostly five and tens. Added up to a hundred and fifteen dollars.

A hundred more than what he'd been paid the first time he hurt someone. Charles Dunstan. Age nine. A total prick. Even then. In the three decades since, little Charlie D had earned himself a fancy degree, had broken a bunch of laws concerning international financing, and was currently served ten to fifteen at a white-collar prison in upstate New York.

He should have hit him harder that day. Might have knocked some real sense into him.

Trout looked at the painting. He had been struggling with the interplay between the blues and the grays. It didn't feel right, regardless of what Dahlia had seen. There was something missing.

With a sigh, Barton Trout tucked the money into the pocket of his jeans. He wiped off his brushes and emptied the jars of water he had been using. He packed his brushes and paints into a canvas bag. After folding up the easel, he carried it and the bag in one hand, the painting in his other.

"It's missing something," Reese said. She took another step back and cocked her head. "Yeah, it's definitely missing something."

The painting was on a display stand in her office. The afternoon sun poured in through the west-facing windows, and the light deepened the blues and washed out the grays. The rock was a dark blotch, an angry fist jutting out of the spray.

"Are you done with it?" Reese asked.

The best word to describe Reese Montgomery was "lithe." Her legs were long; her fingers were slender and shapely, and they reminded Trout of his brushes; her face was the sort of face that was difficult to render in watercolor—capturing her cheekbones alone required a palette knife. Her eyes were blue-gray, a color that Trout saw often but could never quite capture on a canvas.

Trout looked out the window. "Yeah," he said. "I suppose I am."

Reese was quiet for a moment. "I'll take it, of course," she said. "We should call this your 'Quiet Period.' Kind of like Picasso's Blue Period."

"Whatever works," he said.

Trout tucked his hands into his pockets, and his right hand closed around the wad of bills Dahlia had left him.

Reese didn't know Barton Trout—she would challenge anyone who claimed they did—but she knew him well enough to know the difference between his *I'm not thinking about anything* face and his *I'm not thinking about a* very *specific thing* face. "What is it?" She asked, fully expecting him to tell her he had been contemplating eternal nothingness.

"I had a visit from Dahlia while I was painting," he said.

"Dahlia?"

"Yeah, lives in the brown house at the end of the road." Trout put his hand out at mid-chest. "About *this* tall. Rides a red bike. Likes some sort of sports team."

"Some sort of sports team?" Reese echoed.

"I don't know which one. They've got an 'M' in their logo."

"Oh, okay. That's a baseball team."

"Yeah, okay." He nodded. "Baseball. That's it." He looked at the painting, but he didn't see it. His gaze was somewhere else. Somewhere far from here.

Reese was comfortable with these silences from Trout. If she was being honest with herself, there was something about him that was . . . interesting. If she had to guess, she thought he was in his early 40s. He wasn't tall. He wasn't overly broad shouldered. He was fit, but not aggressively so. He wore simple clothes—t-shirts, jeans, dark jackets—and his watch wasn't expensive, but it was very practical and well-cared for. Yes, in fact, those were words that described Trout: *practical and well-cared for.*

She did not know what he did for a living, or, rather, what he had done for a living. She knew he lived in the little cottage at the end of Marbletop Lane. The house was on the wrong side of the road for an ocean view, and it was more than thirty years old, dating from a time when properties in Yarrow were modest and single-story. In the last decade, many of the houses along that stretch of Whitefold Cliff had been significantly remodeled, with one or two stories added.

The previous owner of the cottage had been a retired history teacher from Seattle. Her husband had died a year or so before she bought the place, and she had been content to smell the sea air and work in her little garden of succulents and drift-wood art. Reese had liked her. She always came to openings at the gallery.

Until she didn't, and two months later, Trout had wandered in her gallery with one of the show announcement postcards. He had apologized about telling her that Mrs. Wiggins no longer lived at the address printed on the card. After glancing around her gallery, he said he didn't mind if she kept sending the cards, but could she update the addressee?

*And what name shall I put on file?* she had asked.

*Barton Trout,* he replied.

*Seriously?*

*Wasn't my choice,* he said. *But it'll do.*

She had laughed, and he had joined her.

Later, when she had been having a drink at the Whisk, Elsie Kitteridge had mentioned that she had seen the town's most mysterious resident visiting her gallery. *Oh, you mean Barton Trout,* Reese had said.

*Is that really his name?*

Which was how Reese had learned that he had been in town for a few months, but no one knew his name.

Anyway, it had been a year now, and Reese felt like her gallery was one of the few places Trout frequented when he came into town. They talked about art mostly. He brought in a canvas now and again. She took them on consignment. They sold quickly, as if the paintings were a series of clues that would unlock the mystery of the man who lived in the tiny cottage with the succulents and the driftwood.

"So, Dahlia . . ." Trout said. "Kid *this* high. Lives in the house—"

"At the end of your street," Reese finished for him. "Likes the Mariners. Rides a red bike. Yeah. What about her?"

"Good kid, I suppose."

"I suppose," she said. "Her mom died a few years ago. Some kind of accident. Her father—he took it—well . . ."

"What?"

"His name's Crawford Colton. He and I were in school together, back in the day."

Trout looked at her. She found herself turning away, suddenly unwilling to let him look her in the eye. "We dated," she admitted. "Briefly." She felt her stomach spasm. "Very briefly."

"What's he do now?"

Reese shook her head. "I don't know. After Janice died—"

"Janice?"

"Dahlia's mom."

Trout nodded, as if he understood the story Reese was outlining for him, a familiar set of players in an old tale.

"After Janice died, he didn't work. There was some kind of settlement. I don't really know the details. And he was injured too, in the accident. Afterward, he . . . he . . ."

Trout waited for her to continue.

"He's at the Whisk a lot—Old Whisker's Bar and Grill, over near the Baxter. He doesn't work there, but he's always there, you know? People stop by and see him. He takes meetings, for a lack of a better word. With folks who don't live around here. And the staff . . . well, the staff . . ."

"They treat him like he owns the place, even though he doesn't," Trout said.

"Yeah, like he's important somehow."

"He probably is," Trout said. In his pocket, his hand tightened around the bills Dahlia had left him.

Old Whisker's Bar and Grill was named after a catfish. Or maybe its namesake was the man who had caught the catfish. No one remembered, really. Or why a stuffed fish that was not indigenous to the area was mounted over the bar. *The catfish is part of the indelible charm of the place*, a newspaper man had once said in an article about tourist destinations for folks looking to get away from the city. The bar was a slab of polished teak that supposedly came from a nineteenth century whaling ship. The vintage vinyl booths were from a casino in Las Vegas, rescued the night before the building was torn down—one of the many landmarks which had been wiped away in that relentless hunger for something shinier and sparklier. There was a wine cellar that went deep; some say there was a door down there that led into old smugglers' tunnels.

It was attached to the Baxter Building, the old hotel which had been glorious once, but that glory had faded—perhaps around the time when a handful of men in dark clothing had loaded vinyl booths into the back of a truck, one summer night out in the desert. The Baxter was what they called "mixed use" now: boutique and antique shops on the ground floor; small business space on the floor above; and the upper floors continued to confound a revolving parade of developers who kept trying to build luxury apartments.

Trout wouldn't go so far as to say that he liked the pair of buildings—they reminded him too much of a world he had left behind. Rather, let's say they were comfortable to him. He knew his place in the world they represented. He knew business was done in back booths and private meeting rooms.

Yarrow was a long way from that world, and it hadn't been by accident that he had ended up here. He was—what had his case officer called it?—*cocooning* himself. Wrapping himself up in the slow somnolence of this seaside town so that, in a season or two, he could emerge again. Like a monarch butterfly. Or a death's head moth.

His case officer hadn't appreciated the latter. But then, no one had much of a sense of humor in those days. They were shell-shocked, trying to forget what had happened.

Trout felt the old electricity shoot up his arms as he walked across the parking lot in front of the Whisk—the name the locals used for the bar. The charge started in his fingertips, darted up to his elbows, and then pumped through his biceps and triceps. His shoulders dropped and his back stiffened. Anyone watching him would have seen the subtle shift: a lengthening of his stride, a longer swing of his arms, his hands open and loose.

His body certainly remembered the old days.

Trout pushed his way into the bar, and his focus immediately narrowed. How many at the bar? How many at the tables? Where were the exits? Was there muscle? How attentive were they? Who was liable to be a distraction? Spotting. Marking. Calculating risks. Making assessments.

He went up to the bar and took a seat one stool away from an old fisherman, who leaned against the bar when he picked up his glass with a quivering hand. The bartender, a woman whose top was tight and short, sauntered over and raised an eyebrow.

"Coffee. Black. Real sugar, if you have any," he said.

Beside him, the fisherman cackled, and the bartender shot him a glance. "Coming right up," she said.

The old fisherman looked at her ass as she walked away, and Trout let his gaze wander past the man. On the far side of the room, there was a party of four in one of the bar's historical booths. Two men, two women. The ladies were window dressing, and they looked bored. The men were talking quietly, their heads leaning toward one another.

The bartender returned with his coffee and a small dish with sugar. "You want to start a tab?" she asked.

Trout pulled the bills out of his pocket. He put a pair on the bar. "His next one, too," he said, nodding toward the old man.

The bartender touched her lip with her tongue. "He won't go home with you that easily," she said.

Barton gave her a tiny smile. "It's early," he said.

She shrugged like that didn't matter.

The coffee was hot and strong. Trout added the right amount of sugar, and sat and sipped his coffee awhile. Around him, the other patrons grew bored watching him sit at the bar and do nothing. Their attention wandered. Voices rose and fell. Glassware clinked. The old fisherman laughed at a fleeting memory of a big fish he had once landed.

At the booth, the two men finished talking. One man left, and judging by his expression, the meeting hadn't gone well. Or maybe he was sour about the fact that he was leaving alone.

The women were bored, and as Trout glimpsed the bottom of his cup, one of them slid out from the booth and approached the bar. She hopped up on the stool between Trout and the fisherman, and her skirt was tight around the top of her thighs. Her hair was frosted; her lips and nails were cherry red; and her eyes were shiny with booze and boredom. "Buy me a drink," she said, showing Trout her teeth and her cleavage.

Using a knuckle, Trout nudged one of the bills on the bar.

She pouted. "That's all?"

"Tell me about your friend," Trout said.

"Who? Sally? You wouldn't like her."

Trout shook his head. "Not her," he said. A glimmer of something passed through the woman's eye. Not quite fear. But an animal wariness.

"He's not my friend," she said.

The bartender came over, and when Trout looked at the woman sitting next to him, she shook her head, suddenly uninterested in having him buy her a drink.

"Thanks for the warning," he said.

He stood up and walked toward the booth in back.

It took Crawford Colton three days to talk himself into testing what Trout told him that night in the Whisk.

Trout was at the scenic turnout again, making another attempt to capture the light. The sky was a swirl of white and pale blue. The ocean alternated between a rich blue sway and a slick steel color. *It was the rock,* he had decided. He had been painting it too dark. It needed to be more ephemeral, as if the spray was making it vanish.

He heard the heavy engine of the Mustang as it rolled into the lot. The car coughed once when Colton turned it off, like the tired wheeze of an old fighter as he staggered back to his corner of the ring. The car door slammed, and Colton walked heavily across the parking lot.

He sounded as out of shape as he had looked in the bar.

Trout had walked over to the booth and stood there. He stared at Colton, reading the fine sweat on his skin, the paunch underneath the cheap jacket, the thick joints of the fingers. Colton started off peeved, became flustered, and then got angry. *What the fuck are you looking at?* he had shouted at Trout.

*You want to hit someone, hit me,* Trout said. And then he walked out. Simple as that. All the while thinking about the taste in the back of his throat that had nothing to do with the coffee and the sugar.

Colton stopped behind Trout. "Hey!" he said loudly.

Trout put down his brush. He picked up his cloth, wiped his hands, and slowly turned.

Outside, in the light that stripped away all pretense and illusion, you could see other differences between the two men. They had started similarly, once upon a time, but one had made different choices. And while it could be argued that those choices had lead to certain luxuries and pleasures, they had also lead to regret and anger. And now, when it was too late to make any difference, that anger was all that was left.

"What the fuck were you talking about?" Colton snarled.

"When? Oh, at the bar the other night?"

"Yes, you dumb shit. At the bar."

Trout worked the rag across his thumb. "I thought I was pretty clear," he said.

Colton fidgeted. Colton glanced around like he was sure this was some kind of trap. Colton put his hands together, thought about cracking his knuckles, but then realized he didn't really know how. He deflated a little, and for a brief moment, Trout thought that was going to be it. But then the anger—that fire that had been gnawing at his gut for so long—the anger flared.

"Stop," Trout said. He put up his hand in case Colton hadn't understood him. "Hang on a second."

Colton, his hand half-formed into a fist, froze.

Trout turned his head slightly and looked out past the wooden railing that kept sightseers from venturing too close to the edge of the bluff. "You see that railing there?" he asked. "Here's the thing: you think you're going to beat the shit out of me. I can see it on your face. But I'm going to toss this rag"—he waved it at Colton—"and it's going to confuse you. And then, I'm going to step out of the way, grab your shirt, and hustle you right over to that railing. Maybe you'll fall over it. Maybe I'll have to help you. Maybe you'll hit the ground hard, and that'll be that. Or, maybe you'll do some sort of silly pratfall, the sort of roll they taught you to do at football practice—you did play, didn't you, Crawford? Anyway, you'll congratulate yourself on remembering how not to get hurt when you fall, but it'll be too late, because you'll have rolled yourself off that cliff." Trout shook his head. "It's a pretty stupid way to die," he said.

Trout watched Colton's eyes dart to the railing, back to him, and back to the railing. He watched Colton shift his weight. Clench his fists. Unclench his fists. Lick his lips. He watched Colton come to a decision, and he sighed.

When Colton charged, Trout didn't step out of the way. He didn't throw the rag. He merely leaned back from the other man's wild swing, stepped inside, and caught him flush on the chin with an uppercut that stopped him in his tracks.

Colton dropped like his legs had wandered off without him. He rolled around on the ground like he was a child's top. His eyes darted left, then right, and then rolled back in his head. He panted like a dog.

Trout watched him, and when Colton calmed down, he nodded. "We clear?" he asked.

Colton shook his head, snarling like a feral animal. He started to get back up.

Trout hit him again. And again. And again. Like he had Charlie D back in the day. Like he had so many others. In and out of the ring. Never out of anger. Never for personal reasons. Always for money.

Because that was the one thing Trout was good at.


"This is better," Reese said later that afternoon, looking at the new painting. "I like the bit of red. It makes you wonder what happened. It tells a story."

She smiled at Trout. "Maybe you'll tell me some day," she said.

He kept his right hand in his pocket. His knuckles were swollen. He had finished the painting with his left hand. The splashes of red around the rock were wild and scattered.

"Maybe," he lied.

※

# Hecate Hemlock

# THE HOBBYIST FINDS A PROJECT

"It's a babysitting job." GeeGee pouts because he feels like he has to beg.

"Oh, is that it? I'm your babysitter now?"

He flushes at the thought. "It's just for a few days," he says. "Guy's white collar. Probably never even stubbed his toe or anything. It'll be a piece of cake."

I glance at Vic, who is standing behind the bar. "Cake," I echo.

"It's never a *piece of cake*," she says.

Karine, the day waitress, wanders up with an order, and Vic moves off to help her.

I lean against the bar and give GeeGee a very practiced stare. Honest. Fifteen minutes every other morning. It is a very good stare.

It is also completely wasted on him.

Georgio Gonzalez is five-seven—five-eight in those fancy shoes of his, another inch or two with his hair. He wears off-the-rack suits with wide lapels, like he gets all his fashion tips from reruns of 70s cop shows. Not that GeeGee is a cop. He's a bail bondsman. Every now and again, one of his clients doesn't stick around to watch the wheels of justice do their thing. That's bad for Freedom For All Bonds—Incorporated, mind you, because while GeeGee's taste in TV shows was dodgy, his business acumen was not. A client no-show means a forfeiture of the bond.

Anyway, GeeGee—we all call him GeeGee because what else do you call a guy who is half-Italian / half-Mexican?—is worried one of his clients might do a runner. Thg guy's name is Julius Hanshaw. Arraigned a few weeks ago for possession and conspiracy to distribute a variety of narcotic substances. Prior to his arrest, Julius Hanshaw's claim to fame was being the catcher for his law firm's intramural softball team. When he wasn't getting his glove pounded, he worked on corporate contracts and commercial real estate holdings. The real sexy stuff.

"Come on, Cat. I'm telling you. He's a pastry puff."

"So why isn't McGinnis doing it?" McG was GeeGee's go-to skip tracer.

"He's out of town."

"Since when you do offer vacation days?"

"Family stuff," GeeGee says.

"He's got family?"

GeeGee sputters and makes hand gestures that are supposed to be some kind of explanation, but all I see is a puppet show without any puppets.

I glance at the paperwork again. Hanshaw's booking photo is a middle-aged man in need of some grooming tips about his wispy brown hair. Big ears too. He's doing that myopic shrew face people make when they've been told to relax and look normal for a photograph. A dark bruise marks his left cheek. Must have run into a door or something.

I check my calendar. Trivia night tonight. Open mic tomorrow, which means a visit from the historical beat poet society. Those guys are a handful. Lots of turtlenecks and passionate wordplay about fighting the establishment, along with bad rhymes and navel-gazing. I wasn't a fan.

"Yeah, okay," I say. "I can give it a few days."

"Just through the weekend. That's all."

"That's all?"

"He's supposed to be in court on Monday. You know how it works. If he fails to show, I lose the bail money." He makes puppy eyes at me. "Come on, Cat. Please? Standard skip trace rate. Plus five percent."

I scoop up the folder with Hanshaw's information. "Stop that," I say. "It does not look natural on your face."

Vic fixes me with a knowing glance. I give her a *Do you really want me around for the poetry slam?* eyebrow; she replies with a nod that reads *Watch yourself.*

*Always do, Auntie,* I think as I leave the bar. *Always do.*

My name is Hecate Hemlock.

No, it's not the name I was born with—no one even remembers if I had a good girl name, the sort of name birth parents give a child. I was raised in an ultra-classified military program that created super assassins. It was a Cold War initiative that had its inception in—well, it doesn't matter. Funding disappeared. People who knew about the program died. A lot of paperwork got shredded. Our secret assassin academy was so far back in the mountains, it was easy for us to forget about the rest of the world.

Until we hit puberty and realized escaping a mountain hideout was exactly what we had been trained to do. So, we did. It took us a week to reach the nearest town, four hours to get into trouble, nd two more hours to show the townies they had made a series of bad decisions. As the place burned, we realized we had two choices: go back into the mountains and never come out again, or figure out how to disappear.

Conveniently, we were trained to do that too.

Anyway, I've been in LA long enough now that my tan doesn't fade in the winter. I live with not-my-real-aunt Vic. She owns a bar a long way from the beach. I do security work for her friends, and occasionally I remind the college boys who come to the bar that they should keep their hands to themselves.

I haven't killed anyone in about five years. I should get a pin or something for that.

And sometimes, when I am bored, I let myself get talked into working for people like Georgio Gonzalez. I donate the money I make to the community arts center in town.

I'm not telling you this to make me look like an upstanding citizen. I'm just saying that I believe in the arts, you know?

They're an important outlet for kids. I would have turned out differently if I had had an art class or two.

In the building where Hanshaw lives, there's a name brand coffee shop, a natural food shop filled with boxes and cans, a sports bar, a sandwich shop, and an art gallery. The last one is disappointing. It features locally-sourced art, which means a lot of terrible watercolors of seascapes, driftwood dioramas, and earrings made from seashells.

As I stand in line for a coffee, I check out the building's leasing office. There's a young woman sitting behind a desk, and she has that *I am in a Hell of my own making* glaze on her face. No one wanders in to rescue her during the time it takes for my coffee to be made—which isn't a long time, but it wasn't a short amount of time, either. It confounds me how these fancy coffee places have transformed a simple process into something akin to a ballet company performance.

Anyway, leasing office girl visibly switches on when I push through the glass doors. "Hello," she chirps. "How may I help you today?"

I practice mirroring her facial expressions as I let her give me the sales pitch. I play dumb and blonde long enough to get a look at the floor plans, and I promise to come back later with my man—*oh, he makes all the decisions; I'm no good with money.*

I use her key card to access the upper floors of the building. She never even noticed that I took it.

Hanshaw's unit is on the eleventh floor. GeeGee's notes says that he shares it with a woman. Girlfriend, lover, sex toy: GeeGee didn't know. What he did know what that she didn't show up to post bail. *So, not married and not engaged,* I summed up when GeeGee told me. *Got no ties to him.*

I hope she's not around. I put the odds about fifty-fifty—not that it would change my approach. It'll be easier to sit on Hanshaw if I don't have to deal with a gold-digging harpy.

*Maybe they're taking it slow*, GeeGee countered when I used that word. Half Italian / Half Mexican, remember? He's a big softie when it comes to romantic stories.

Anyway, the unit is a little over twelve hundred square feet, which wasn't outrageous by local standards, but it's palatial compared to what I grew up with. The unit faces south, which means, on a good day, you can see the Santa Monica Mountains.

Today is not a good day, but few are, anymore.

The kitchen has granite counters and stainless steel appliances. An enormous television takes up half the living room. There are two bedrooms, and the smaller one contains a desk and an embarrassing assortment of home gym gear. A bench. Some free weights. Tension bands. A couple of yoga mats. Weekend workout equipment.

Judging by the clothes I find in the main bedroom's walk-in closet, the girlfriend / lover / sex toy—the *harpy*—is in charge of the relationship. There are a few nice pieces, but they're several years out of fashion, which says she makes the rounds at the discount ranks.

I totally called it. She's in it for his money.

Hanshaw has a half-dozen suits in varying shades of blue and gray—work clothes—along with a bunch of bowling shirts. He must be in—what?—a dozen leagues? Weird, but hey, I can think of a lot worse hobbies.

I check out the nightstands, curious what sort of games the lady of the house is into. The contents are disappointing, and I cross "sex toy" off my mental list. She has a book of trashy erotic short stories, and I make myself comfortable on the bed and read one.

I'm at that point in the story where the cable guy's friend shows up when I hear a distinct 'click.' A dead bolt turning sort of 'click.'

I mark my place in the book with a finger and listen.

The front door opens and then closes. No other sound follows.

It's not the girlfriend. I've seen her shoe collection. She couldn't sneak up on a dead badger. Nor is it Julius. He's not the creeping around the house type. Especially his own house.

That means someone has broken in. Another snoop! How exciting!

I put the book back in the drawer and, silent as a moth, pad over to the bedroom door.

The hardwood floor in the living room squeaks as the intruder gets nosy. Kitchen drawers are opened and closed. The hall closet is checked. He goes into the bathroom, and I hear him look in the medicine cabinet and—*oh, good for you!*—the toilet tank.

I forgot about the toilet. Such a classic spot for hiding contraband.

I hear two squeaks from the hall, and I realize this is a two-person job. One of the pair goes into the office / home gym, and the other approaches the bedroom.

I take a peek at him through the gap between the door and the frame. About six feet tall. Gray jacket and stocking cap. Jeans. Goatee, along with a scruff of stubble. What is it with men who hassle with cultivating a bit of fur around their mouths, but don't bother with upkeep elsewhere? Is it supposed to say *I'm fashionably lazy, but still dude enough to grow facial hair?* Maybe I could ask him after—

Hold on. Let me take care of this.

I punch him in the kidney as he enters the bedroom. He grunts and folds up, shifting into a defensive stance. I grab the back of his collar and slam him against the wall. He makes gargly noises, and when I kick him in the knee, he twists, stumbles, and goes down.

I'm in the hall when his pal comes out of the home office. He's a few inches shorter. Same outfit. Same grooming failure. Bigger nose, though, which I smack with the flat of my hand. A follow-up strike to the throat thoroughly confuses him. While he's sorting out what happened, I bounce him off the wall too. Then, knee strike and—

What? I'm being efficient. I'm not trying to impress anyone.

By the time both men recover, I'm in the living room. Space to maneuver. More stuff to throw at them. Easy access to the front door if I need to exit quickly. But I stick around. Maybe they want to chat.

"Whatcha doing, rooting through *my* stuff?" I ask. I stress the possessive, wondering if they'll mistake me for the live-in girlfriend.

Shorty—the one in the hall—is breathing raggedly. His eyes are red. Squirrel Tail—because that is what his goatee looks like—decides he wants another go. "Where's your boyfriend?" he snarls as he pushes past his friend.

Score one for me. That acting seminar I took last month is totally paying off.

"Who's asking?" I shoot back.

They look at one another, unprepared for my response. Shorty wheezes and waves a hand to say that he's deferring to his pal. Squirrel Tail advances, hands outstretched. When he's close, I grab the nearest finger, bend it in the wrong direction, and kick him in the leg again when he yowls.

What? I wasn't going to let him put his dirty hands on me.

He tries to hit me, but it's like watching a 747 make a right turn on the runway. I duck under his swing, and—I've still got his finger, remember? I haven't broken it, yet. I duck and pull his arm as I go. It's kind of adorable how he hugs himself.

But not so cute that I don't knee him in the balls.

As Squirrel Tail drops and moans like a seal with sunstroke, I tuck away a strand of hair that has escaped my thrown-together updo. "How about you?" I ask Shorty. "You having fun yet?"

"Fuck you, bitch," he says. He pulls a gravity knife out of his jacket pocket and flicks it open.

"Really?"

His answer is to wave the knife. I feign distress and back up. He steps around Squirrel Tail, who is still quite blue in the face. Shorty grins. He thinks the three-inch blade gives him an advantage. He makes his move, leading with the knife.

I was six when I learned how to disarm an idiot with a bladed weapon. It's all muscle memory now. While my hands do whatever it is I've forgotten they know how to do, I'm distracted by a thought about my refrigerator. *Mustard*, I think as I pluck Shorty's knife out of his slackening grip. *I'm out of mustard.*

Shorty squeals about something, and there is blood on the floor.

"Don't slip in that," I warn him as I leave.

When I get to my car, I realize I left my coffee in the apartment. Good thing I used a fake name when I ordered it.


The goons do what goons always do: they bail at the first sign of trouble and run home to Daddy. Squirrel Tail is driving, and his insistent signaling and five miles under the speed limit pace suggests he has reason to avoid drawing attention to their car. Makes it real easy to follow him. I flip through the local radio stations, trying to find something that I can sing along with, as he leads me to an industrial area on the other side of the 101. There are lots of trucks coming and going, and I lose sight of their car. Fortunately, I spot it again as I wait behind a pair of trucks at a stop sign. There. On my right. Parked next to a large warehouse.

I note the name on the building and turn right at the next opportunity. I follow the fence as it marks off a large area, and when I come back around to the building where Shorty and Squirrel Tail went, my count is eight. Eight warehouses.

Blue Spar Limited has quite the operation.

I park across the street and watch the building. After fifteen minutes or so, I figure it's time for me to move on. I'm conspicuous, and I get the feeling the guys inside the fence aren't going to fall for the *How do I get to Universal Studios from here?* trick. I mean, I do it very well, but even though they are probably still getting grilled by their boss, Shorty and Squirrel Tail might have gotten around to telling stories about the crazy chick who cut them at Hanshaw's.

Okay, I only cut *one* of them. Whatever.

I have to be patient. Oh, there's nothing I hate more than having to be patient. But I have more questions than answers— no, wait, I hate *that* more. Anyway, there's nothing I can do at the moment. There's no point in going back to Hanshaw's. He's not going to show up there. *Later*, I decide, *I can come back later*. Do some breaking and entering. The sort of thing every good girl likes to do when the sun goes down.

Midnight. Security at Blue Spar is a trio of guys who make their rounds with the lumbering enthusiasm of lifers who know the inside of the fence is as good as their lives are going to get. It's tempting to spice up their evening, but I catch myself. My boredom isn't their problem.

I ghost through a door in the back of the main building. There will be cameras—three guys can't cover eight buildings—and sure enough, I spot one, clamped to the wall like a wart. It has a fixed field of view. A toddler in a padded walking trainer could slip past it.

There are six more scattered throughout the main floor. All looking in one direction. I could bring an entire dance company through there and no one would notice.

I had spent the afternoon looking into Blue Spar's financials and business dealings. They were a commercial shipping company who did a lot of business with overseas manufacturing. Mostly construction materials and the rest was cheap crap. Knock offs. Seen on TV merchandise. Mall kiosk filler. Flavor of the month health and beauty products. The list was long and boring.

I went looking for building plans instead and found enough to suggest that the main building had administrative offices.

Following the plan I had memorized, I locate the security office. It's always good to know where the goons are eating donuts. I'm surprised to find another pair parked in the office, watching the monitors. Okay, so *five* knuckle-draggers. Not three. And one of them looks like he's actually paying attention to the screens. Ugh. Motivated hourly wage earners are the worst.

I crawl past the office and take the stairs to the upper floor where the boss's office is located. The door is locked, but the panel is flimsy. All it takes is a jiggle and a thump to pop the door. Inside, the room is tastefully decorated (for a shipping magnate who has offices in the Valley, I mean; it wasn't that classy). It's a *Take a Meeting and Look Important* room. There aren't any filing cabinets and the computer on his desk is an after-thought. I can't imagine Boss Man typing in all those product SKUs for hair weaves and plastic clogs.

A couple of bottles of single malt whisky are stashed in the sideboard. I pour an inch into a tumbler and sip it as I examine the huge oil painting hanging on the opposite wall.

The Scotch is pretty good. I leave the bottle on the sideboard, thinking I might take it with me. After I crack the safe behind the painting, of course.

How did I know there was a safe? There's always a safe in the *Take a Meeting and Look Important* rooms. It's mandatory decor.

The painting is a ginormous snowscape. It's at least six feet long and a couple of feet high. There's a building in the foreground that I feel like I should recognize, but either the artist wasn't very good or they had taken a lot of liberties. So many hedges.

Thankfully, the frame is mounted on a swivel and the whole thing swings out from the wall. Behind it—surprise!—is a shiny metal door with a combination dial. It's a Bungelmeiser. A 2500. If I were a girl who was easily impressed by security hardware, I'd be, well, *slightly* titillated.

Aunt Vic has a 525, one of the compact models that were used in railway cars back in the day. Bungelmeiser, like many security companies, sticks with what works, and I could open the 525 with one hand while wrestling with a baby goat with the other. The 2500 shouldn't be too hard.

I time myself. Two minutes thirty-eight seconds. Not bad. Would have taken thirty seconds less if I had remembered to spin the dial all the way around five times before I started. One of the quirks of the Bungelmeisers. *Getting soft, Cat,* I think as I open the safe.

The safe is bigger on the inside than the outside, and I lean in to check out the contents. Cash. Bearer bonds. A couple of pouches that make *I'm filled with precious stones!* noises. There's a cedar box that holds an antique 1911 Colt Revolver with mother-of-pearl inlays on the grip. Nice looking gun, but man, so big and heavy. The sort of gun that announces your arrival. *Boom! Hello honey, I'm home!* A box in the back contains data CDs with cryptic notations written on them.

I take two of the CDs, along with one of the pouches of stones.

It's only when I close the safe door that I notice the security plate on the inner frame. There's a matching plate on the door. When I opened the safe, I tripped an alarm.

Whoops. Definitely getting soft.

There's only one way out of this room, and it's the same door the security guys are going to use.

I throw a regretful glance at the bottle of Scotch. *Sorry about that,* I think. *Maybe next time.*

Boots are loud on the stairs as I leave. I feel the familiar tingle across my shoulders and in my legs as adrenaline kicks in.


"What are these discs?"

I gesture at the data CDs on GeeGee's desk. "I don't know," I say. "That's why I brought them to you."

He wasn't happy to see me. Okay, I had been sitting on his bed when he woke up, and I may have spooked him with the flashlight under the chin trick, but whatever. I wasn't happy with him either. Once he got over being home invaded, he had noticed my stern face and knew that I knew that he had lied to me.

You don't lie to the babysitter. That's, like, rule number one. Or maybe rule three. I don't know. I don't babysit, remember?

Anyway, we're in his office. He, in a heavy robe with a dragon emblem on the back of it; me, with an ice pack for my cheek and a bottle of gin I found in the freezer for my attitude. I had dumped the data CDs on him. I hadn't said anything about the bag of diamonds.

They were definitely diamonds. I wasn't going to donate them to the community arts center. Not because they wouldn't have appreciate my generosity—*oh, these stones will pay for a lot of craft supplies!*—but because community arts people are terrible at fencing hot rocks.

"You should put one of these discs in your computer," I tell GeeGee. "That's why I brought them here."

"What's wrong with your computer?" He scrunches up his face as I put my feet on his desk.

"It's at my place," I say.

He continues to scrunchy-face as I juggle the ice pack, a glass, and the gin. I manage to get booze in the glass without spilling any—a testament to the four months I toured with a traveling circus as part of a deep cover job in some country I shouldn't name. I sip the cold gin and stare at GeeGee. He sighs and switches on his computer. While it does its computery thing, he fusses with his robe and steals glances at the bottle cradled in the crook of my arm.

"Get a glass," I say. "You know where they are."

"I'm fine," he says curtly.

The computer finally comes to life, and he puts one of the discs on the sliding tray. He shoves the mouse around on his desk, clicking with passive-aggressive ferocity. "It's a bunch of files," he says. "Spreadsheets. Projections." He shakes his head. "I don't know what any of these names mean."

"Accounting." I sigh and empty my glass. Hair weaves and plastic clogs and stuffed rhinosauruses. Ugh. "Accounting is so boring," I say out loud. Then I giggle.

He looks at me like I've lost my mind.

"Rhinosauruses," I say.

"What about them?"

"It's a funny word. I like funny words." I say it again, adding an extra 'us' or two. He doesn't see the funny, which only makes him grumpier about being woken up at two in the morning to look at stolen spreadsheets. He focuses on the screen, and after moving his mouse around for a bit, he puts his head at an angle. A thinking crease appears on his forehead.

"What?" I ask.

"You're not—" He frowns. "I think it's a . . . park . . . ?"

"A what?"

"A theme park." He pauses. "For kids."

That gets me out of my chair. I peer over his shoulder. Sure enough, he's found a model drawing for a proposed theme park, and judging by the names on the rides, it is for the kids. The document is an extensive proposal: budget, architectural renderings, scale models, five- and ten-year business plan. The whole thing. GeeGee hits a section that is plat maps and land surveys. It's all parcel numbers and grid lines, but each page has a notation in the corner. Latitude and longitude.

GeeGee scratches his chest. I can tell he's thinking, but he doesn't know his geography as well as I do.

"West of here," I say. "Fifteen miles or so. Near the 101 and Calabasas."

He gives me a look.

"What? I'm very good at geo-spatial location," I say.

"That is not a thing."

"It is totally a thing. They have satellites that do it."

"You're not a satellite."

I give him a *So nice of you to notice* look as I push his hand away from the mouse. "How are they getting this land?"

"Isn't that National Park land or something?"

"Or something." I fly by long sections of legalese until the pages turn into columns of numbers. "Here we go. How much is this going to cost?"

GeeGee and I stare at the number at the bottom of the column.

"Wow," he says.

"Yeah," I say.

"Where did you find this?"

"A warehouse. In Sherman Oaks."

"And what does this have to do with . . ."

"The guy you sent me to babysit? The guy who wasn't home? The guy who has done a runner?"

"Whoa. Hold on now."

I put my hand on his shoulder and squeeze. Not enough to hurt him. Just enough for him to know I could. "Don't annoy me," I say.

He twitches under my grip. "Okay, okay."

I gnaw on my lip as I go back to scanning the document. So much legal jargon. How can anyone read all of this? "Who did Hanshaw work for?" I ask.

GeeGee fumbles through the stacks of folders on his desk, finds Hanshaw's, and opens it so we can both look at the summary sheet again. "Law firm," he says.

"In Sherman Oaks," I say. I scan the box where GeeGee noted Hanshaw's official job title. "Huh. Real estate work and commercial holdings."

We both look at the business plan document on the computer screen.

"That's a lot of real estate," GeeGee says.

A *lot* of real estate, and now, damnit, more questions again. Is this a real business plan? Did Hanshaw write part of it? Did he think it was a bad idea?

More importantly: what did any of this have to do with the three keys of cocaine that were allegedly found in his car?

"I don't like questions," I say.

GeeGee makes a sputtering noise and fiddles with the edge of his robe. Always helpful, that one.

I tell GeeGee to print out a copy of the business plan, which takes longer than either of us wants to be sitting around and staring at each other. Finally, the three hundred page document finishes, and I haul it home with me. I have good intentions, but after two shots of good American vodka and twenty minutes in a hot bath, I really don't care about plat maps and real estate transactions. I'm asleep as soon as my head hits the pillow.

Sunlight wakes me, which is terrible news, because my bedroom faces west. I struggle out from under the blankets which have entangled me during the night. My watch says I missed most of Thursday. Even if I skip my morning—well, *waking*—workout and don't do anything with my hair, I'll still be in rush hour traffic. That thought almost sends me back under the covers.

I persevere. A cold shower helps. It puts a dangerous glint in my eye when I finally show up at the bar.

Vic gives me a once-over with a raised eyebrow. Her conclusion is to fetch a cup of coffee. She yells at Darius, the cook, for a "Benny Special." He loudly complains that they stopped serving breakfast six hours ago.

"It's for Cat," she says.

"Of course it is," he shouts.

"He's just grumpy that he has to make a new batch of hollandaise sauce," she says.

"I can have a burger," I say.

She gives me the grandmama look that says she will brook no such nonsense from me, and I acquiesce. I mean, I *could* have a burger, but Darius's Eggs Benedict are—and I'm not trying to sell you anything here—transcendent. I'm out of sorts, but I'm not stupid. "Thanks, Vic."

She notices something on my face and ducks her head slightly so she can get a better look at my left cheek. My hair's down. It—and a slap-dash-running-out-the-door layer of makeup—hide most of the bruises. Thankfully, the swelling in my lip has gone away.

"You play with the wrong crowd last night?"

"It was a narrow hall and it got a little crowded. Plus, they weren't very good about taking turns."

She makes a dismissive noise in her throat. I don't blame her. The security guys at Blue Spar had been rude and crass. It had only been a pair at first, but two more showed up before I could finish. I didn't kill anyone, but I definitely broke some bones.

Hopefully, Blue Spar Limited had decent liability insurance. They were on the clock when these "workplace accidents" occurred. It was the least I could do.

"It wasn't as much of a 'piece of cake' as GeeGee said it was?" she asks.

"I don't even like cake," I mumble.

She gives me a *I told you so* eyebrow. I ignore her look and drink my coffee. It is hot and it burns away the remnants of last night's dead-to-the-world slumber. One more cup of this and a plate of runny eggs and Darius's hollandaise sauce will make everything better. *Ready to take on the world!*

Or, at least, go find a legal aide who had pissed off a greedy commercial magnate with grandiose dreams of creating a wonderland for tots.

Oh, I know. So many questions.

Vic shakes her head. "You've got that look," she says when I protest. "Whatever it is, it's not your problem. Do the job. Don't get involved."

"Something not right here."

"No, Hecate, you've got it backwards. *Many* things are not right. You're the one who keeps thinking it—*any of it*—can be fixed."

"People shouldn't get hurt for things they didn't do."

"You don't know that. You don't know anything about this guy. He may have done exactly what they say he's done."

"So why did a pair of heavies toss his place? What were they looking for?"

"Didn't he have drugs in his car?"

"And they hadn't heard that the cops had picked him up already?" I shake my head. "Come on, Vic. Don't be like that."

Vic has the good grace to acknowledge my point with a twitch of her shoulders. "So what it is then?" she asks.

I blow out my cheeks as I think about where to start. "Well, there's a theme park with rhinosauruses and—"

"A theme park?"

"With rhinosauruses," I say. I tell her the highlights of the plan. I may have added the rhinos.

Vic frowns. "GeeGee know about this?"

I haul out the three-hundred page document out of my bag and drop it on the bar. "He knows," I say.

She flips the page edges. "What did he say?"

I duck my head. "He told me to find Hanshaw," I mumble into my coffee cup.

"And this?" She flip-flips the document.

"It's . . ." I slurp coffee loudly.

"It's a distraction," she finishes for me.

I put my hands on the bar. "I'm bored." God, listen to the sound of my voice.

Vic ignores the whining noise. "You need a hobby," she says.

I sit up straighter. "I have one!"

She narrows her eyes. "This is not a hobby," she says, indicating the business plan.

"Why not? It's just like one of those comic book stories. I have a mission. It's for the kids!"

"Those are fantasy stories for adult men who are afraid to talk to women," Vic says.

I pout. "But . . ."

She doesn't want to be drawn in by my big lip, but it's a very pronounced lip. "What?" she says.

"Aren't I one of those fantasy stories?"

She snorts. "I am sorry I ever told you about that, Hecate."

"Okay, fine. Would you rather have me hanging around the bar tonight, heckling the poets during their open mic?"

"No," she says strenuously.

"Then I'm going to make a nuisance of myself somewhere else."

Her lips twitch. "I wish you wouldn't say it like that," she says.

"Don't wait up for me."

"Don't call me collect."

"Never," I swear.

She shakes her head as she wanders off. She knows if I get picked up by the cops that I'll call her lawyer, Handsome Bob. He's the one who can shake a toy poodle out of a cop's mouth when they've got their jaws locked.

His name's not really Handsome Bob, by the way. On his very fancy business cards, it says "Robert Edward Stalwart, Partner." His father founded the firm—Stalwart & Associates—and they are very expensive and very exclusive. Handsome Bob has very few clients: Vic, the bar, a guy in Burbank, and, well, me. I call him "Handsome Bob" not because it is true—though it is—but because it makes it him blush.

Vic is right about Blue Spar. It is a distraction. But I can't help but be curious as to why they are so eager to find Hanshaw. When I get curious, I get a special tingling feeling.

No, not *that* tingly feeling. Don't be weird. I'm a professional. Not a pervert. Well, okay, maybe on the weekend, and only if my date is amenable to trying new things, but that's not what this is. Not at all.

*Focus, Cat,* I think. *Find your man. Track him down before the bad guys do.* Except I have no idea where to look for him.

Well, hang on. What was it he had in his closet? Bowling shirts. He had lots of bowling shirts.

Who has a dozen bowling shirts?

Well, guys who like to bowl is who.

Pretty good, huh? See? I told you I was a professional.

☆

There are over twenty bowling alleys in the Valley. I have a headache from all the noise and fluorescent lighting by the fifth. Two drunk guys try to pick me up in the parking lot of the eighth, and the eleventh reminds me so much of a decrepit diner in Budapest that I stay for one drink. The place smells of rot and wood smoke and industrial plastics, and the bowlers are all men in their sixties who look like they haven't the slightest clue about bowling. They chatter in German and French; one of them is an old Czech spook who is so tired of hiding that he can't be bothered to disguise his accent anymore. Shrapnel in his left hip puts a hitch in his stride, but if he shoots a rifle like he rolls a ball, he must be deadly at five hundred yards. Totally adorable. I seriously consider adopting him.

It's after ten by the time I hit number fourteen on my list. It's closed, but there are lights on. Three cars in the parking lot, and over the next fifteen minutes, employees come out of the bowling alley and drive off in the cars. I sigh and cross this one off my list. As I'm checking my street map for the best route to the next place on my list, the side door of the bowling alley opens and someone comes out. They toss a pair of trash bags into the dumpster and go back inside before I can get a good look.

I sit and wait. The building is mostly dark. It doesn't get any darker. It doesn't get any lighter. No one leaves.

Whoever is inside is planning on staying all night.

Gee, who does a sleepover at a bowling alley?

I wait ten more minutes. Cars pass. No one shows any interest in the bowling alley.

Time for me to get some answers.

The hinges of the side door squeak, and there is an emergency crash bar on the inside, like you see on the doors in school cafeterias and movie theaters. I try to ease it quietly into place, but it is fussy, and it clacks loudly when I release it. Great. Why don't you tap dance across the lanes while you're at it, Cat?

Machinery in the kitchen hums and gurgles. Wood groans somewhere in the building. A HVAC starts up, and a light breeze caresses my cheek as I crouch behind a ball return station.

Wood groans again. *Upstairs,* I think. It's dark, but I can see enough to note that the ceiling is lower over the back half of the building. There's a mezzanine. I make my way across the bowling alley, looking for a door. A flicker of reflected light catches my eyes. Someone is coming. I drop behind a rack of bowling balls as they reach the bottom of a set of stairs on the far wall. They have a flashlight, but its beam is weak. The ball return station near me is illuminated briefly as they sweep their light around the room.

I wait. They wander across the room. When I am confident they are past me, I dart around the rack. The last place they'll expect to find me is upstairs. I'll be a fun surprise.

Hanshaw makes a noise like a buffalo having a seizure when he finds me in his recliner a few minutes later.

"Surprise!" I say.

"What the fuck!" he manages. He hasn't shaved since his booking photo, and the bruise on his face has turned sour. He's wearing a food-stained t-shirt and a pair of sweatpants a size too large. The look in his eye says he's wishes he was a chicken.

"Don't," I say. I point at my feet. "I'm wearing good shoes. I'll catch you before you get halfway across the parking lot."

"Fuck," he says. His shoulders slump. He looks like he wants to have a good cry. He gestures aimlessly with the flashlight in his hand. "Are you . . . ?"

"Am I what?" I'm not helping him out.

He exhales heavily. "I didn't tell them," he says.

"Tell who what?"

"Aw, man. Don't be like that."

"No, seriously. I don't know what you're talking about."

He opens his mouth, closes it. He looks around, wondering if I'm the only surprise waiting for him.

"It's just me," I tell him. "And I don't work for Blue Spar."

His shoulders jerk, and the panic wiggles down his spine and makes his knees wobble.

"Wow," I say.

He sits down heavily at the dinette. "I never should have looked at that document."

"The plans for the theme park?"

"I didn't—" The panic wiggle makes another circuit under his skin.

I put up my hands, like I'm trying to calm a cornered animal. "It's okay. I really don't work for them. Or"—I struggle to figure out who else might be involved—"Or *them*. Neither of them. Okay?"

He's still not convinced. "Then . . . why are you here?"

"You were arrested. Someone posted bail for you," I say. "And you scampered."

"You're . . . you're a bounty hunter?"

I make a face, even though—technically—he's right.

"Look, I don't know anything about anything," I say. "I was hired to find you because, yeah, GeeGee's a bit concerned that you might make him forfeit the money he posted."

"GeeGee?"

"Freedom for All Bonds. The guy who got you out of jail."

"Oh, that guy." He looks apologetic. "I, uh, I have his card somewhere."

"It's okay. You don't have to check in with him. You just need to show up for court."

"But I didn't do it," he protests. "Those drugs weren't mine. They were planted in my car. Those fuckers at Blue Spar. They think I leaked the documents."

"Hey, it's okay. You don't have to convince me. I'm just—"

His lower lip trembles. "You're here to make sure I don't run."

"Yeah," I say, somewhat apologetically.

"I'm not running," he argues.

I glance around the room. There are two windows: one, covered with a heavy curtain; the other looks out over the bowling lanes. A small refrigerator is tucked into a corner, and a toaster and a hot plate take up most of a nearby counter. The dinette set looks like salvage from a kid's playroom. The recliner leans to the left. The bed is a cheap mattress on top of a slab of unfinished pine which is on top of a bunch of milk crates. The TV is older than me, and the rabbit ears are covered with crumpled tin foil. As hideouts go, it's not the worst, but . . .

Hanshaw hunches his shoulders as I give him a judgy look. "Are you going to sit there and watch me?" he asks.

"Yup," I say.

"From now until . . . ?"

"Monday morning," I say. "Your court appearance is at nine."

"But . . . ?"

"What?"

He frowns, looks at his hands, sighs. "Nothing," he says. He looks like he's found a dead rodent in his pocket.

I silently ask Vic for forgiveness, but not too strenuously. "Fine," I say. "Tell me what happened."

"I'm innocent," he says. "The drugs aren't mine."

"Don't turn this into one of those after-school TV specials," I say.

Once he finds his rhythm, the story comes out quickly, like water rushing out of a bucket when you punch a hole in the side. The surprise twist isn't Blue Spar, it's the other guys. The other *them*. An Eastern European crime syndicate. Some left-over bunch of Communist Bloc hardcases. Albanians, probably.

The theme park is a chunk of the story, definitely, but it's really all about turf—who has control of what and where. And Hanshaw, bumbling law firm filing clerk, spilled Blue Spar's secret plan to the wrong people.

And there it is: the whole cake.

Hanshaw sees me grimace. "It's bad, I know," he says. He fusses with his hands.

"It's not—well, okay, yes, it is, but . . . I don't like cake."

"What?" He looks at his refrigerator. "I don't have any cake."

"It's not important."

"I might be able to make one . . . they probably have everything you'd need in the kitchen . . . downstairs."

"It's a metaphor," I say.

"Oh, okay."

"In fact, it's not even cake. It's more like . . . baklava."

He fidgets. "Which isn't like what . . . ?"

I give him a glare, daring him to talk more about baked goods. He reacts to my look—the one I've spent all that time practicing. And don't think I don't notice and appreciate his effort.

"What . . . what are you going to do?" he asks.

"We are not having any baklava, that's for sure."

I hear Aunt Vic's voice in my head. *Adopt the old Czech. He's house-broken. He won't make much of a mess.*

I lean forward and give Hanshaw one of the smiles we had been taught by our finishing school instructors. *I'm a very pretty girl, aren't I? You want to take me home, don't you?*

Hanshaw squirms and that look of total panic creeps into his eyes again. He doesn't like my smile.

*Stay out of trouble,* Vic says in my head.

*I'm just adopting a stray,* I tell her. *It's not my fault if other people—*

*Don't,* she warns me.

But it's too late. I have found a project.

✳

# Butch Bliss

# COLD KISS

I met Huggy Bear a week or so after I got out of jail.

A production company had blocked off most of the street and the parking lot of the Ralphs off Santa Monica in Westwood. There were a dozen police vehicles scattered around the lot—most of them were sporting colors and decals that weren't quite right. They had left off "Protect and Serve," for one. Hollywood sleight-of-hand. You're supposed to think *Oh, this takes place in LA* when you see a show on TV, and it works for all the markets that aren't within a hundred miles of LA's sprawl. The locals know, however. They know they don't have to get nervous about how much grass they're carrying; they don't have to wonder if there's any white powder still dusting their nose. No one cups their hand around the mouth and nose and does a quick alcohol test.

Hollywood does its best to not annoy the locals, because it's hard to get outdoor location shots if the locals are restless.

This production company knew what they were doing, however. They had us far back from the action. You could barely see the camera set-up.

"I can't see a damn thing," said a short guy standing next to me. He was wearing a Dodgers ball cap, a tracksuit with a familiar logo on it, and sleek sunglasses that he thought made his face look leaner. They didn't.

"There's nothing to see," I said.

He glanced over at me—well, glanced up at me. I had a good eight inches on him, and I'm rarely the tallest guy in the room.

"You wanna put me on your shoulders so I can see for myself?" he asked.

"You got fifty bucks?" I replied, thinking that would settle the matter.

It did, but not in the way I expected.

He drew a crisp hundred dollar bill from a wallet made from some kind of shiny leather. It wasn't cow—too slick—and it looked unnaturally soft. "And you get me closer," he said, holding out the bill.

It was, frankly, more cash than I had to my name.

"Sure," I said. "Five minutes, though."

His fingers darted into his wallet again, producing a second bill that looked a lot like the first. "Ten," he said.

"Okay," I nodded. "You got yourself a ten-minute pony ride."

He was polite about it. He didn't bounce. He didn't pull my hair. He didn't turn it into some weird *Thunderdome* homage. He was, however, heavier than I expected.

He spotted a gap in the tape, and we made it to one of the long trucks. I leaned against the front tire of the rig, and he peered over the hood. "Oh, I knew it," he gushed. "*Beach Patrol.* I love this show."

There had only been one TV at Tehachapi, and it got one channel, on a good day. We stayed abreast of the daytime soap operas, because the Mexican Mafia liked to talk about the naughty things they would do with the actors and actresses. Occasionally, we'd get a ball game, though we'd rarely get through the whole game without a fight breaking out. Other than that, I read in my cell, worked out in the yard, argued with Dicky Boy and Tattoo Bob, and did tai chi with Mr. Chow. A real model prison, that's me.

I glanced over my shoulder. We were a couple of miles from the beach. Not that such real world details mattered in Hollywood. There was at least one Ralphs closer to the water, but it probably didn't have the right vibe to it. Maybe it was facing the wrong direction, and the afternoon sun would have cast weird shadows. Maybe there were too many palm trees along the edge of the lot. Satisfying the director's vision was the location scout's problem, and again, every market outside of LA wouldn't know the difference.

I hadn't always been this cynical. *A cynic is a man who pisses in his own water,* Mr. Chow used to say, *and then complains about the taste.*

I blame the California Department of Corrections and Rehabilitation. Mr. Chow had a saying assigning blame, too. Something about you can't blame a tree for being a tree. Whatever. I always ignored him when he went full Zen monk on us.

My new friend tapped my head. "Let's get closer," he said.

I shrugged, letting him know how precarious his position was. "Let's not," I said. "Your time's almost up."

"Two hundred more," he said. "For five more minutes."

I shook my head. "This is wandering into a thing that neither you nor I are going to be thrilled to tell our friends about."

"I don't have any friends," he said.

I had a smart reply all lined up, but it died in my throat.

"Come on," he whined. "I want to see Lolita Brigade."

He was vibrating, his thighs buzzing against my ears. It wasn't a weird sexual thing (thank God for that), but it was something deep and visceral, a yearning that went way beyond a *I'm spending some private time in my room with my posters* sort of obsessive behavior.

And truthfully? I felt a strange affinity—an unquantifiable sense of simpatico-ness—with him.

"I don't have any friends either," I said.

He struck a quick *pat-pat-pattity-pat* on my head. "You do now," he crowed. "Come on, Small. Let's go see the girl."

I didn't move.

"What?" he asked.

"My name isn't Small," I pointed out.

"I know," he said. "It was, you know, never mind."

"I do mind. I read a story once about a guy and a puppy." I shifted him on my shoulders. "Things didn't turn out well for that puppy."

"Maybe—maybe you heard me wrong. Maybe I said . . . I said something else."

"I'm sure you did," I said. "Like 'Bliss.'"

"All right. Come on, Bliss. Let's go see the girl." His heels tapped against my chest.

I still didn't move.

"Oh." He realized what he had done. "Sorry."

"Don't push your luck."

He quieted down and said nothing more until after the production spotted us and chased us off the set. Then, red-faced with laughter about the whole thing, he had stuck out his hand and introduced himself. Hugh Gene Bartholemew, but everyone called him Huggy Bear.

He was my first friend in LA who wasn't in the movie business, and for a few weeks, it was a nice change of pace.


"I'm sorry Mr. Bliss, but Edgar Baylor is no longer with the firm. We have a case file of his efforts on your behalf during your case with the City of Los Angeles, we don't have any records of a storage unit."

This conversation took place a day or two before Huggy and I met at the *Beach Patrol* set. I know I'm telling this out of order, but my brain was a little scrambled after a week of listening to Huggy talk about *narrative pacing* and *breaking the act structure* and *hitting your emotional beats. It's all about how you tell the story,* Huggy said. *You gotta keep the audience in the dark, but you also have to give them something. Some kind of information drip.*

Or something like that. Anyway, let's back up for a second. After finishing up my ten-year stint with the California Department of Corrections and Rehabilitation, I came back to Los Angeles. I spent that first afternoon with a few old friends. We agreed that ten years was a long time—none of us bothered to keep in touch—and well, *Gee! Is the afternoon over already? It was good to see you and all, but . . .*

The only other person who might have cared that I was out of prison was part of the letterhead at Trent, Baylor & Howe— though, ten years on, it was just Trent & Howe now. Edgar Baylor Sr. had died a few years back, and Edgar Jr., the one saddled with defending me against the City of Los Angeles, had decided against filing the old man's shoes.

The guy glossing me off was Donald Martins, the poor bastard at the firm who got stuck with the hard cases who wandered in. Martins was doughy in the face, and either his collar was too tight or his tie was strangling him. Or maybe it was the fact that he was talking to a real *Honest to God!* ex-con that was making him all flushed and sweaty.

"Well, gee, Don—you don't mind if I call you 'Don,' do you?—what do you think happened to all my stuff when I went upstate?" I asked.

He flapped the folder on his desk. "I don't know, Mr. Bliss. It's, uh, not in your file."

"Do you know what happens to people whose trials go badly?"

Don gave me a blank look.

"You haven't done much pro bono work, have you?" I guessed.

Don cleared his throat, trying to find a polite way to tell me that his fancy law degree—the one hanging on the wall behind him, in fact, all nice and presentable in its shiny frame—meant he wasn't supposed to deal with the losers and degenerates who couldn't afford their own counsel.

I saved him the trouble of putting all that into words. "I don't suppose you have a number for Edgar Jr?"

"Actually—" Don shook his head. "I'm sorry, Mr. Bliss. I can't help you."

"Can't say I'm surprised," I said. My first few days of being a free man had been "confusing." "Aggravating" also came to mind. As did "Fucking Bullshit," but as Mr. Chow used to tell Dicky Boy when he got in a particular snit in the yard: *Cursing never opens doors or unlocks opportunities.*

*May get a girl to open her legs, though,* Tattoo Bob pointed out. *Isn't that right, Butch?*

I tried to stay out of these sorts of conversations, but there were only so many places you could hide in the yard.

Anyway, prior to enjoying the custody of the State of California, Baylor Jr. had assured me he would make sure all my shitty stuff in my shitty apartment would get packed up. *It'll be in storage, Butch,* he had said. *Waiting for you when you get out in a couple of years. Don't worry about it.*

Of course, a "couple" turned into a decade because of an incident in the shower and a subsequent plea bargain down to Involuntary Manslaughter, but who was counting? I hadn't heard from Baylor after my re-sentencing. Pro bono work doesn't pay the bills, after all.

"All right, Don," I said to the dough-faced lawyer with the sad puppy look. "Obviously I should take a shit on your desk as a way of saying thanks for all the marvelous work the firm has done on my behalf."

Don flushed even pinker, and he had trouble forming words. Was I was the first ex-con to threaten to defecate in his presence? That was something, I guess.

I didn't, however. Mostly because being free had left me a little *not-free*, if you know what I mean. Change in routine does that to a man. Makes him all tense. His natural cycles are all off. His chi gets disturbed.

I could see why convicts found reasons to get back inside when they got out. The world was a cold place. In prison, you knew where you stood. You knew you were going to get fed. You knew when it was bedtime. You knew when to avoid the showers. All that structure makes sense to Johnny Ex-Con.

But I wasn't going back in. I had done my time. I didn't owe anyone a thing. No, wait. I literally didn't own anything.

Talk about being free.

The trouble was: what was I supposed to do with all this freedom?

Doing pony rides for overly enthusiastic fans of television celebrities had netted me some cash, but it wasn't something I was going to turn into a habit. Still, I celebrated with a room at the least skeevy hotel in West Hollywood that still accepted cash. The bed was only marginally better than the cot in my cell, but the air conditioning worked. There was a continental breakfast, and I lingered over a third danish and a second cup of coffee, considering my options. Well, my option—singular—which was: stay out of prison.

Sure, I could rob a convenience store, and sure, I could walk into the ocean, but those were defeatist choices. The flush of freedom was still on me. I had a positive mental outlook, and before it all drained away like soap scum in the shower, I should bolster that outlook. *Tai chi is all about movement and flow,* Mr. Chow told me when he first started teaching me in the yard. *We are meant to be in motion.* Even when you were locked up (somewhere like, say, CDCR's facility in Tehachapi), you learned how to move within the limitations of your environment. Even when the guards put you in the Hole (not that such a place officially exists at Tehachapi), you kept moving in your mind. You kept flowing.

After breakfast, I hit the streets and made a half-hearted attempt to be a responsible citizen. By mid-afternoon, it was pretty clear what my options were: Zero, zip, and nada. I was unemployable. Even to wash dishes. Being an ex-con gives you a stain that, ironically, no amount of industrial cleaning product and hot water wash could get out. I wasn't deterred by this realization—positive mental outlook, remember?—but it meant I would have to consider non-traditional employment opportunities. Thinking outside the box sort of opportunities.

I enjoyed thinking outside the box. I had been inside one for too long.

I spent the night several blocks east of my previous lodging, and there is—let me tell you—a not-insignificant difference

between half-a-star and no-star in hotel rooms. I slept in the
tub, using my jacket for a pillow. It was the only area in the
room that had been recently cleaned.

The following day, fortified by a cheap cup of convenience
store coffee and a bran muffin, I signed up for a studio lot tour.
I wandered away from the tour group the first chance I got,
thinking I might slip into a crew—one of those guys who was
happy to fetch stuff and move things around. If I pulled the
trick off for a week, maybe I could convince them to put me
on payroll because I had been useful, right? Wasn't that how
someone famous got their break in Hollywood?

Lot security was all about crushing dreams, however, and
I got noticed within the hour. A quartet of guys with shiny
badges and polyester uniforms warned me that if I ever came
back, they'd have me arrested for trespassing and harassment.
My picture went into a folder labeled "Stalkers." That was
apparently a thing now. People are weird.

I had about thirty bucks left and fuck-all for prospects. Sure,
there were people in the business I could look up, but after the
party I had crashed with Tex my first afternoon out of jail, it
was possible that might be more trouble than it was worth. Not
to mention I really didn't want to get back into that life.

*Keep moving forward,* Mr. Chow said. *Don't look back.* In the
direct-to-cable movie of my life, this was a forty-five second
backstory montage with a voice-over. And backstory, while
useful, wasn't forward motion. You had to keep the story moving.

And so I called Huggy.


I found a bench that looked out on the Los Angeles River and
watched people for an hour. It was still a novelty. In prison,
you learned to be aware of everything without actually looking
at anything. It was nice to not have to wonder if the young
mother with the stroller was going to stab me with a sharpened
bedspring.

Huggy showed up in a dust-colored Jeep, and he quickly cleared the maps and the Thomas Guide from the passenger seat before I got in. "I appreciate this," I said.

"Yeah, yeah, no problem." Huggy wheeled us back onto the 101, and we eased our way into thick traffic. "Did you have a meeting or something?" he asked.

"No, nothing like that. I was just sight-seeing."

"Yeah? Which studio?"

I told him which lot. "They shoot a lot of network shows there," he said. "Did you see anyone famous?"

"No," I admitted. "I didn't." I tapped my fingers against my leg. "To be honest with you, I wandered off. Got caught."

"What? How'd you manage that? They keep a close eye on those tour groups." He said it with the conviction of one who knows.

"It's nothing," I said, disliking the idea of talking about why I had gone to the studio. "It was a dumb idea."

"Oh, man. Were you stalking someone?"

"No, I wasn't stalking someone. I don't even know who is supposed to be on that lot."

"Sure, sure." Huggy's head bobbed up and down.

"You don't believe me."

"No, man. It's—like—whatever. I get it. I really do."

I thought about him riding my shoulders at the *Beach Patrol* shoot the other day. "What about her?" I asked. "You stalking her?"

"Who?"

"That gal from *Beach Patrol*?"

"Lolita? No!"

I didn't believe him. The silence got awkward between us, and Huggy broke first.

"Okay, okay," he said. "I'm not stalking her, but I'm keeping an eye on her."

I gave him a *Sure, and you'll get points on the back end in that movie deal* look. "You paid me a couple hundred bucks for a pony ride the other day," I said. "Just to get a better look."

"Yeah, well, it was a good idea. There was a crowd."

"It's okay if you like her. She doesn't mind—well, within reason, I mean. It's part of why people get into the business. They want to be seen."

Huggy gave me a shrewd look. "You're in the business, aren't you?"

"I was."

"Was?"

"I took some time off, and now . . . Now I'm not sure if I want to get back into it."

He screwed up his face. "It's Hollywood," he said. "Why wouldn't you want to be in it?"

"It's complicated."

He waved a hand at the surrounding gridlock. "We've got time."

I could have told him—maybe I should have—but the concrete albatross of my past was an exhausting weight. I wanted something new. I had done my time. I shouldn't have to be defined by that period of my life. "I've been away," I said, glossing over the last decade. "Working out of town. That gig ended, and for lack of anything better, I thought I might come back and see if there was anything here for me. I guess."

"You guess?"

I rolled my tongue against the inside of my cheek. "You know how you love something for a long time and then you learn it isn't good for you? Like donuts or cigarettes. You want to stop eating donuts, but man, they taste so good, don't they? You've gotta figure out a way to change this behavior. You gotta stop yourself, but that's really hard."

Huggy nodded thoughtfully. "Donuts," he said.

"Yeah, donuts," I said.

Huggy gave me a *I'm not sure if you're really talking about donuts, but I got you, man* look. "I like pie," he said.

"What?"

"For me, it's not donuts. It's pie."

I wasn't sure if he was being serious or if "pie" was code for something else. My brain defaulted to the meaning every twelve-year-old boy snickered over, and I tried to work backward. If "pie" meant that, what did Huggy think I had meant about "donuts"?

"Cherry pie." He licked his lower lip. "Boston creme pie. Pecan pie. Oh, man, a good apple pie? That's the best. And the berry pies! Those are dope. Strawberry rhubarb pie. Boysenberry pie."

"Okay, okay," I said. "It was a crap metaphor."

"Hey, I'm just talking about pie here."

I smiled at him. "Yeah, well, fuck you and your pie fetish."

He laughed, and I joined him. The shared moment cleared the air between us, and Huggy seized the conversation and took it in an unexpected direction.

"I think she's in trouble," he said.

"Who?"

"Lolita. I think someone actually is stalking her."

I could reference Lolita Brigade's namesake—*light of my life, fire of my loins*—but this was the sort of poetic nonsense Huggy mooned over late at night when everyone was asleep. *My sin, my soul.* But to get lost in such purpled passion would be to acknowledge that Deirdra Betty Montauck had any idea what you were talking about. She wasn't a fan of books; if pressed, she would admit to reading *Variety* and *The Hollywood Reporter*. Maybe one of the gossip mags when they ran a story about one of her peers who she—not so secretly—wished would fall off the Santa Monica Pier and get eaten by a shark. The *Beach Patrol* writers never bothered with long monologues. They knew her fans tuned in for the slow-mo beach shots.

*I like lollipops,* she once said when asked about her name. Pressed to comment further, she said—and this is the actual quote: "From that film, you know, the one about the guy who goes crazy and chases the girl around with an ax."

*Poe-ta-toh, pah-tato.* This was Hollywood. At least she got the director right.

Anyway, Deirdra—Dee to her mother, Dahling Lolo to her manager, and *Lo-Lee-Ta* to her adoring public—was a sex symbol for a new generation raised by TV. She knew a coquettish double-entendre was better for ratings than genuine emotion and that plot was secondary to wet t-shirts. She was perfect for a show like *Beach Patrol.*

A cross between a police procedural and a spring break documentary, *Beach Patrol* was a phenomena that defied the critics and industry pundits. The major networks had turned their noses up at it, and the premium cable networks had balked at its budget. The producers sold it directly into syndication and licensed it to a hundred countries, where it became the cultural touchstone by which most of the world judged America.

It was a Hollywood star-making machine. Young men and women with generous physical assets who could look thoughtful while wearing very little were in demand after a guest spot on *Beach Patrol.* A three-episode arc was a solid guarantee that you'd land a minor speaking role in next summer's action blockbuster.

Watch the first season of the show. Look for Deirdra in an early episode. She has one line, and her character senselessly dies like all young women do in television—Hollywood's cheap way of showing the audience how warped the villain was.

Her episode was exactly like a hundred other hours of television, but someone in the writer's room liked Deirdra. They weren't ready to let her go. Her character's death turned into lingering trauma that haunted one of the mains. By the end of the reason, Ricky Boston—played by hunky mall poster boy Hutton Chandler—was obsessed with dead Deirdra. So, too, was the audience.

And when Lolita Brigade showed up in the last minute of the last episode—a dead ringer for the character killed eighteen episodes earlier—the fan base lost their mind.

The producers and Lolita's manager spent the summer denying the actress from the early episode and Lolita Brigade were the same person. No one really believed them, and when the new season started, the press had other things to chew on.

Ricky Boston died at the end of the second episode of season two, saving Lolita Brigade, of course. Naturally, she tearfully declared she was going to dedicate her life to saving others, because that was what Ricky would have wanted.

Huggy insisted we watch all three and a half seasons. *We can't be friends if you're not a fan of* Beach Patrol. Since I was sleeping on his couch, it was hard to say no. And yeah, watching the show wasn't the worst way to spend the evening. Better than, say, wrapping oneself in cardboard under the overpass.


Huggy's zealousness about Lolita revolved around two basic facts: 1) She was a goddamn movie star, and her talents were wasted on the small screen; and 2) he had written a script that would show the world what he knew about her. Of course, if some crazed fan—not Huggy; no, he was her secret protector—kidnapped Lolita or stabbed her or did something equally bizarre, then she wouldn't be able to star in his movie.

This was Hollywood logic, of course. He wanted to *help* her. That made him a *good* guy. Whoever this other person was, they wanted to *posses* her, and that made them the *bad* guy. I was pretty sure this was a plot out of any number of straight-to-video train wrecks—ninety minutes of romantic suspense you weren't supposed to think too hard about.

Most of us haven't read Nabokov's book either.

Anyway, I stayed at Huggy's, where I was fed a steady diet of Huggy's world view. Abstractly, the parallels between learning to love the world like Huggy did and sticking to Mr. Chow like an attention-starved puppy weren't lost on me.

A handful of scenes for every episode of *Beach Patrol* had to be shot on the beach (or near enough that you could see the beach), which meant a fairly regular schedule of location shoots. And if you were a fan of the show—which was a significant share of the 18-24 year old demographic, thank you very much—it wasn't hard to find out where the crew was on any given day.

Today, that was the boardwalk at Venice Beach. We parked several blocks away and worked our way through the crowds. It was a beautiful day, even by California standards: the light was good, it wasn't too warm, the wind off the ocean was blowing the smog inland, and the whitecaps made the water look properly cinematic.

They were filming a "walk and talk"—a scene where actors attempt to do those two things simultaneously. It can get complicated, especially when a director thinks this was a chance to show off how many times they've seen Scorsese's *Good Fellas*. Actors have to learn dialogue *and* blocking. Hit this mark *here*. Say this dialogue *here*. Turn forty degrees *here*. Walk over *there*. Say more dialogue. Even with a good cast and crew, these setups can be time-consuming. More so when you are shooting on a live location.

Anyway, what we saw when we finally got to the barricades was a bored crew who were in "hurry up and wait" mode.

"What's going on?" I asked a guy who had been rubber-necking for awhile.

"Aw, man. You missed it," he said. "One of the actors lost his shit. He was yelling at the director. It was pretty awesome."

I glanced around, looking for the talent. There were a half-dozen trailers parked in the lot next to the boardwalk. A variety of crew with headsets and clipboards hovered nearby, like bees queuing up to get back into the hive.

The guy saw where I was looking. "Yeah. That front one? That's his trailer."

"His?"

"Timothy Grifton. He was the dude who was yelling."

"Oh, right, right."

Timothy "Griff" Grifton was the show's leading man. Before landing the role of Lieutenant Marshall Black, Beach Patrol's tan leader, he had been a professional surfer. Chiseled abs. A perfect cleft in a perfect chin. Blue eyes. Black hair—not too long, not too short. Much like the shadow on his cheeks: not so bristly that he'd leave whisker burn, but enough to suggest he hadn't sleep in his own bed last night. The right amount of gravel in his voice and the right amount of smolder in his gaze.

Half of *Beach Patrol*'s viewing audience thought he was a dumb pool boy who had—somehow—convinced a lot of people he could swim and solve crimes. The other half—the larger portion, frankly—thought he was dreamy.

Perfect casting, in other words.

Next to me, Huggy fidgeted. He was wearing a light blue track suit. I had seen his closet. Track suits were all he had. Under the top, I knew he was wearing a t-shirt that was a replica of the shirt worn by the Beach Patrol team. "Who else is in the scene?" he asked the bored guy.

"Brigade and some dude."

"Anyone famous?"

The guy shrugged. "Nah."

"Cool, cool." Huggy fidgeted with the zipper on his track suit. I knew what he was thinking: hop the barricade, lose the top, pass as an extra.

I nudged him with my shoulder and shook my head.

He gave me a *What? I'm just a guy, waiting for something to happen here* sort of look.

I was spared having to respond. The door of the front trailer opened, and God's gift to water and women stepped out. Not far from us, a couple of women shrieked his name, and Grifton was savvy enough to smile and wave as he strode toward the camera setup.

PAs scurried to the other trailers, alerting the talent. More people popped out of trailers, but Huggy and I had eyes for only one actor.

Lolita Brigade walked with a ragged masculinity—the sort of stiff-legged bounce you often saw in fresh convicts. Hher outfit was a short jacket, a teal blouse, and a pair of gray slacks. Her shoes weren't entirely sensible, but she was only walking and talking, so it didn't matter. She had burgundy highlights in her hair. It was shorter this season, a sexy pixie cut but a little long and shaggy, like she was a month overdue for a salon visit.

The other person in the scene was a character actor dressed in a shabby suit. He hadn't shaved in a week and his hair was professionally mussed. His gait changed as he approached the camera setup. He developed a limp and he hunched forward like he was sore from having been recently kicked in the kidneys by a donkey.

As the actors gathered at a designated spot, a handful of extras got into background positions on either side of the camera set-up. A frumpy looking fellow with frizzy hair and an oversized sweater wandered over to the monitors.

A hush crept through the crowd of fans. The locals were well-trained. They knew when to shut up during a film shoot.

The kid with the clapper did their thing, and the scene started. The camera rolled down track next to the boardwalk. The three actors walked. A young woman in very short shorts and skates came along the boardwalk. Griff, talking animatedly, turned. His hand nearly whacked the skater in the face. Instinctively, she ducked. Local talent. You had to know how to dodge and weave like that if you were going to skate along the boardwalk.

Unfortunately, the whack and weave weren't what the director wanted to see. He yelled "Cut!" Lolita said something to Griff, who, in turn, said something back, and that started another round of the argument they had been having before we showed up. The character actor limped back to the starting marks and hung out, like he was a marionette who was waiting for his next cue. The director slumped in his chair, hands over his face.

"They've been trying to get this scene for an hour," the guy next to me said.

"It's not like watching it on TV, is it?" I said.

He shook his head. "Nah, man. It ain't like that at all." He worked something in his mouth.

"Why are you out here?" I asked.

He gave me a *You must be one of them damn tourists* look.

"Right," I said. "Silly me."

It wasn't hard to understand his expression. He and I and a couple hundred other people were standing around—wasting daylight, as the saying went—simply for the opportunity to see a TV star in the flesh. Fame was a strange thing. It fed you. It made you more than you were. Many of us were eager to chase it. Spend our whole lives doing so, if we could. We'd grab it greedily when we had the chance. Lament endlessly when it was gone.

When I had been shooting movies, we worked less publicly. We shot with a very small crew, in a location that was rented (or borrowed, even), and we worked as fast as we could. And acting? No one cared. I couldn't recall a time when a director came back with notes about how well we had read a line or if we had showed true emotional depth in a scene. Hell, most of the time, my face wasn't even on camera.

In contrast, the *Beach Patrol* crew was juggling not only a mercurial cast, but also weather and daylight. Everything the actors did—on and off camera—was visible to the watching fans. A thirty-second scene could take three or four hours to get right. It wasn't an exciting process to watch.

I turned to Huggy and found someone else standing beside me. About the same height, but she had long blonde hair and dark sunglasses.

"Your friend went over the barrier," she said, noticing the look on my face.

"Of course he did," I said. I recovered and offered her a smile.

She smiled back. "I'm Sarah." She offered her hand. "You a fan?"

"Butch," I said. Her grip was surprisingly firm. "I'm learning how to be a fan."

"It's pretty easy," she said. "You just have to show up."

"I hear that is true for a lot of things in life."

She dipped her glasses and let me see her eyes. I smiled again, letting her know I liked the eye contact. Someone shuffled through the crowd behind us, and I moved as a body brushed against me. We were now six inches closer. She didn't seem to mind.

"What do you do, Butch?"

I thought about my response for a moment. "This and that," I said.

"Recreationally?"

"Professionally."

She laughed. "You're one of *those* people."

"Which people?"

She shook her head. She wasn't going to give up that secret so easily. I nodded smoothly, letting her know that I knew she knew. Now that we both knew, there was a connection between us.

In my head, I heard one of Mr. Chow's prison yard aphorisms: *The trick to being invisible is looking like you belong right where you are standing.*

The crew finished resetting their equipment, and as the actors returned to their marks, Sarah turned to watch. Her shoulder brushed my arm, and I felt her lean back as the director called for the cameras to roll.

This time, Griff managed to not smack the roller-skating extra. The three actors walked and talked. The director called out "Cut!" The AD said something, and the crew dissolved into a flurry of activity.

"It looks like they got the scene," Sarah said. "Finally."

The dude standing nearby made a noise somewhere between a hiccup and a grunt. Sarah looked at him and he spooked. I watched him shove his way through the crowd. I felt like I had missed something between the two of them.

Her hand touched my arm, and I forgot about the grumpy fan.

"What are you doing tonight?" she asked.

It felt like a trick question, but I wiggled out of it. "Watching *Beach Patrol*," I said.

She smiled. "By yourself, or . . . ?"

I looked around for Huggy again. There was no sign of him, which was both good and bad news. "By myself, I guess."

"Fans don't let fans watch by themselves," she said. She dipped her sunglasses again. "Unless . . ." Her gaze went up and down.

"I'll be fully clothed the whole time," I said. I knew that look.

"Pity." The glasses went back up. A naughty smile tugged at her lips. "You should join us."

"Us?"

She nodded. "Fans don't let fans—"

"Watch by themselves," I finished. "Yeah, okay."

"Okay." She gave me an address and told me to show up early if I wanted to mingle.

"Should I bring a friend?" I asked.

"Only if you must."

"He's the one with the car," I explained.

"You're very mysterious," she said. She trailed a finger across my arm as she left. I watched her walk away. She didn't look back.

Huggy showed up at the car about an hour after the shoot had wrapped. His face and head were shiny with sweat, and he couldn't stop smiling. "Did you see that?" he said.

"I didn't see anything."

"Precisely!" He indicated the t-shirt under his half-zipped track suit. "No one said a thing about me. I even helped a PA restock water in the trailers. It was awesome."

"You could have warned me," I said.

He spread his hands. "I didn't think you'd want to . . . you know . . . plus I only had one t-shirt."

I shook my head. "It's fine," I said.

"Are you mad about it?"

"It's fine," I repeated.

"You're definitely mad about it."

"I'm not."

Deciding to not press the issue, Huggy unlocked the car. "I have a date tonight," I said as I slid into the passenger seat.

"Really? Tonight?"

"Tonight."

"But it's . . ."

"I know. *Beach Patrol* is on."

"I thought we were going to watch—you *are* mad at me."

"I'm not mad," I said. "Besides fans don't let fans watch *Beach Patrol* by themselves."

"Oh? Oh, *those* guys."

"What?"

He shook his head as he started the car. "You met Phil and Burko, didn't you?"

"No, I met Sarah."

"Sarah?"

"She invited me to hang out and watch the show with her and—"

"And Phil and Burko and the rest of the gang," Huggy finished.

I frowned. "She didn't say anything about Phil and Burko."

Huggy chortled. "Oh, they'll be there."

I made a generous pout.

"What?" Huggy wasn't sure he liked the look on my face.

"Will you drive me to the party, Daddy?"

"Oh, for fuck's sake."

"Please?" I dragged out the second syllable. "You can tell them all about your big adventure on set."

He wrinkled his nose, but he didn't say anything. I had him pegged and he knew it.


The address was in Castle Heights, just north of the 10, and it was a refurbished craftsman with an addition in the back. "It's Burko's place," Huggy told me as he rang the bell. A middle-aged man wearing a t-shirt with a worn iron-on decal answered the door. His smile dropped when he was who was standing on his porch. A frosty wariness colored his eyes.

"Hugh," he said.

"Bernard," Huggy said.

Bernard's eyes flicked toward me. "Who's this?"

"My date," Huggy said acidly.

It was interesting to watch him process that thought. It started with elation, but the joy quickly vanished as Bernard realized Huggy was messing with him.

"Butch," I said, holding out my hand.

And just like that, Bernard's confusion was back.

Huggy pushed past him. "The rest of the gang here?"

"I, uh, yeah," Bernard said. "They're in the Ops Center."

Huggy nodded and wandered off like he was familiar with the layout of Bernard's place. I stayed in the foyer, offering a polite smile as Bernard closed the front door.

"I'm not really his date," I said.

Bernard snorted. "I knew that," he said.

A narrow living room opened off to the right. The couch sagged in a way that suggested you'd never get out of it again. A small television sat on a stand near the picture window. It felt like an after-thought. Movie posters hung on the walls. I hadn't seen any of the films, and I was struck by the fact that they were a concise summary of the decade I had lost.

"I'm a huge fan of the show," I said, dragging myself out of the undertow of nostalgia that was drowning me.

He grunted as he shuffled past me.

"Especially that Vivian Vance lady," I said. "She's really great."

That stopped him. "Who?"

"You know, the neighbor who lives downstairs?"

"There is no neighbor in *Beach Patrol*," he said.

"Oh, *Beach Patrol*." I smacked my forehead. "Sorry, I get my classic TV mixed up sometimes."

He stared at me like I was a loon.

Sarah saved us from more awkward conversation. She appeared in a doorway on my left, a beer bottle in each hand. She was wearing a slinky black outfit that was too sexy for watching TV at home, much less at a friend's house. "Butch!" she exclaimed when she saw me.

"You know him?" Bernard whined.

"I do. Met him at the shoot today." She offered me a beer. "Didn't see you there," she added.

"I had to work," Bernard mumbled. Judging by the look in his eye, Sarah had given me *his* beer.

"Thanks, but I have to do some algebra later." I held the beer out to Bernard. "Is there sparkling water or something?"

He took the beer and made a show of wiping the top with his t-shirt before he took a long pull from it. "In there," he said, nodding toward the door where Sarah had come from. "We're all in the back." And with a *I dislike being threatened by your attitude toward other men, especially when you are wearing a slutty skirt like that* squint at Sarah, he ambled off.

As soon as he was gone, I plucked the beer out of Sarah's hand. "Naughty girl," I said. I took a swig from the bottle.

"What?" She said.

"Bruising the host's ego like that."

"Burko?" She made a noise with her lips. "He just wants to get into my panties."

I took another drink. "You aren't wearing any," I said.

She smiled knowingly. "Gosh, mister. I feel so naked and vulnerable before your piercing gaze."

"You are going to be trouble, aren't you?"

"Of course I am. Now that you are here." She plucked the half-empty bottle out of my hand and strutted off in the same direction Bernard—Burko—had gone.

This time she looked back to make sure I was watching.

✩

The addition in the back was a mini theater / fan cave. An enormous projection TV filled one wall, and four sofas were arranged in staggered rows. On the wall opposite the TV were full-sized posters of the *Beach Patrol* cast, including Ricky Boston, who had died at the beginning of the second season, and Caroline Waxworth, who had left at the end of the third season.

Look at me. Barely three weeks out of prison and I knew all of America's favorite TV characters by name. I could hear Mr. Chow's voice in my head: *Is this what you gave up ten years of your life for?*

*Yes*, I thought, turning my attention to the crowd gathered for this week's episode of *Beach Patrol. Obsessing over something completely inconsequential is the very definition of freedom.*

Two guys sprawled on the front row sofas in a way that reminded me of wild animals marking their territory. I recognized one of them as the guy I had met at the Venice Beach shoot. Huggy stood on the left side of the room, nodding in conversation with a pair in matching t-shirts. Sarah was talking with a young woman with dark hair and glasses. She wore a conservative blouse and a white-washed jeans. I didn't want to indiscriminately label her, but she struck me as the research assistant in the group. The other woman in the room sat on a sofa, having a conversation with a Mexican fellow. The sofa straddler I didn't know was leaning over the back of his sofa, interrupting like douchebags do.

I wandered over to stand next to a familiar face: Lolita Brigade's. Up close, I spotted a hairline crease across her poster, a line running right across her neck. I peeked under the poster and spotted a line of tape across the back.

Once upon a time, someone had razored her head off.

The opening notes of the *Beach Patrol* theme song burst out of big speakers mounted on the wall. Conversation died, and Burko turned the lights down as the show's opening credits sprang up on the projection screen.

We sat and watched. No one talked. It was an oddly formal experience for what was an entirely forgettable mid-season episode. Most of the twenty-two to twenty-four episodes of a season of network television are produced back-to-back. It's definitely a grind, and somewhere around the fifteenth or sixteenth episode, everyone starts to run out of enthusiasm for the work. You're not close enough to the end to start ratcheting tension for the season cliff-hanger. Mid-season sweeps were a few weeks back. This is the spot in a season where episodes won't feature the entire cast, or the producers try out some new writers who stick closely to the defining elements of the show: serial killers, boating accidents, and corrupt politicians. *Beach Patrol* was in its fourth season, and they hadn't gotten to the point in their run where they tried to cram all three of these elements in a single episode. But, oh, that moment wasn't far off.

The only bit everyone remembered afterward was Lolita's slow-mo beach chase. The writers had contorted themselves rather dramatically to get her into an actual bikini (instead of the usual one-piece bathing suit). She ran her suspect down, straddling him like he was a pony as she cuffed him. No one bothered to ask where she had been hiding those cuffs a few moments prior. That wasn't a detail we were supposed to be worrying about.

One of the sofa straddlers, after the credits had run: "Man, she could cuff me like that any day."

Sarah spoke up from the couch on the other side of the room. "Yeah? Is that what your secret sex dungeon is for, Phil?"

Phil flushed. "That's not what it's—that's not what I meant."

"No?" Her eyes were bright with an unexpected gleam. "Maybe a little rough stuff in the back of the car then?"

"Pee break," Burko called out, interrupting the exchange between Sarah and Phil. "And then we can watch it again." He looked at Sarah. "Politely," he added.

She tossed her hair and stomped out of the room. There was an exaggerated sway in her hips. She was acting for the crowd.

More importantly, she was heading for the bathroom in the main part of the house.

I turned to the woman wearing the white-washed jeans. "This place have more than one bathroom?" I asked.

"Barely," she said. She held out her hand. "Gina."

"Butch," I replied. I nodded toward Phil and Burko who were arguing about some deep weeds canonical detail. "How long have you been a part of this group?" "

"This season," she said. "I didn't see you here last week."

"I'm a new fan," I admitted. "Not like some of the people in this room."

She smiled and looked at the posters along the back wall. "Oh, Burko is harmless," she said.

Before I could ask a follow-up question, Huggy wandered over. "Hey, Gina," he said. He stood there, a little stiff.

"Hey, Huggy," she replied. Her voice went a little flat.

And now I had a different question.

"Can I talk to you for a minute?" he asked me.

"Sure."

He touched my arm, indicating we should step away for some privacy. Gina got the hint and rolled her eyes.

"Look," he said when we had retreated to a corner. "This group can get a little . . . bitchy."

"I've been around people with strong opinions before," I said. "I can handle it."

He grimaced, unhappy I wasn't picking up what he was obliquely referring to. I gave him a look I learned from watching cartoons on Saturday morning in the common room at Tehachapi. That slightly vapid, dazed look a coyote gets before a speeding van creams him.

"Sarah used to date one of them," he said.

"Phil?"

"No." Huggy shook his head. "One of the cast."

"Oh," I said. I ran through the cast list in my head. "So?"

"It didn't end well," he said.

"Does it ever?"

"Well, no, I guess, but . . . she's a bit . . ."

"Bitchy?"

He looked past me and blew out his cheeks. "That's not what I was going to say."

"It's what you said a minute ago."

"That was—that was—look, it's not the same thing."

"Okay." I waited for him to explain it more clearly.

He looked over at the group, who were milling around in that way people do when they don't want to look eager, but don't know how to wait without fidgeting. "Not here," he whispered. "I'll tell you later."

"Okay," I said again.

Huggy slapped me on the arm. "Okay," he said. "Good talk."

"Good talk," I echoed as he wandered off.

Not for the first time since I had gotten out, I wondered why I had bothered leaving the comfortable embrace of my six by six room at Tehachapi. *It's always easier to get into bed with the Devil you know,* Mr. Chow used to say.

Speaking of which, Sarah made a beeline for me when she returned to the Ops Center. "You want to get out of here?" A coy smile touched her lips. "I know a place with more bathrooms."

"I'm okay, actually," I said. "I have good bladder control."

"I'm sure you do," she said. She leaned closer. "It's not so much that part I'm interested in. It's the other part."

"Which part?"

"The part that—" She stopped and cocked her head. "Are you really that dense?"

"No, I know what you're talking about," I said. "But conversations like this have been a rarity for me these past few years."

"Yeah? Where were you? Prison?"

"Yeah," I said. "Tehachapi, in fact."

She stared intently at my face, trying to read if I was lying to her. Gradually, a giddy delight bloomed in her eyes. "Really?"

"Really," I said.

"No wonder you knew I wasn't wearing any panties." She grabbed my hand. "Come on. Let's go have some fun."

Huggy frowned as she pulled me out of the room. We made eye contact, and he did a *Son, I'm disappointed in your life choices* head shake.

Tattoo Bob's voice went off in my brain. Not Mr. Chow's. *If the Devil is willing to give me a hand-job, you're damn straight I'm going to get in bed with him.*

I sensed a comeback from Mr. Chow, and I shut down that part of my brain. Sarah's grip was warm and firm. How many days had it been since I'd had some real human company?

*Multiply by ten . . . Carry the one . . .*

Too fucking many.


The club was hidden in an alley off Sunset Boulevard. A slowly winking neon eye crowned an unmarked door, which was guarded by a velvet rope and a pair of doormen with matching muscles. A thick line of well-dressed hopefuls queued like a ragged centipede out to the street. Sarah blew past the line and managed to catch the eye of one of the doormen.

He gave us a once-over and wasn't impressed. Sarah, in her tight skirt, looked classy enough, but I was wearing a well-worn t-shirt—my cleanest one, mind you—and slightly baggy jeans. Hardly the sort of club wear that got you into the posh places. However, one of the secrets of Hollywood is looking like you were famous enough that none of the rules applied. It was on everyone else to recognize you.

Sarah got the guy to approach the rope and she started whispering in his ear. I stood nearby and gave her a *What sort of dump did you drag me to, woman?* look. Someone in line made a noise like they recognized me—God bless 'em—which was the juice Sarah's lie needed. The dark-haired bouncer nodded at his pal, and they let us in. I opened the door for Sarah, and waved to the crowd as she slipped past me.

Inside, it was dark and loud and Sarah kept contact by rubbing her hips against my crotch. I followed her like an attentive retriever. We danced for a little while, though the music wobbled so much I had trouble finding a rhythm. A light show spattered the audience, throwing up highlights of her hair, her eyes, and her mouth.

I had fumbled through the math during our drive to the club. It had been three thousand, eight hundred, and something or other days since I had been this close to a woman. Since I had felt the curve of a hip against my hand. Since I had felt fingernails rake across my forearm. Since I had felt teeth nip at the skin of my throat.

We broke free of the dance floor. She shoved me against a wall, and I wrapped my arms around her. Our mouths met. Her hands fumbled with my clothing. I felt a loosening at my waist, followed by the hot touch of her hand inside my jeans.

I stiffened, pulled her closer, and let my own hands wander. My thumb pressed against her inner thigh and—

She turned her head suddenly, and I got a mouthful of hair. When her hand tightened, I squirmed. "What the—"

"Look," she hissed. The length of her body pressed against me. I turned my head to get my mouth free of her hair. "Look who it is."

I didn't care about anyone but the woman in my hands, but I tried to be polite. I really did. Sarah hadn't struck me as someone who would get all goose-eyed about a famous face while she was having a hands-on moment, but . . . Anyway, I looked around, trying to read faces in the gloom and glitter.

And then I saw the walk. That stiff-legged bounce. That short pixie cut.

"Is that—?"

"It's her," Sarah whispered, her breath hot in my ear. "It's Lolita Brigade." Her hand tightened again.

I made a noise. "Could you—?"

She rubbed her breasts against my chest. "Aren't you excited?"

"I am excited," I said. "Mostly because your hand is being very friendly."

"You're not excited to be this close to her?"

"Her? Lolita?" My voice broke. Out of confusion, not because of anything her hand might be doing.

"You are, aren't you? You are a star-fucker. I knew it."

"No. What?" This was getting awkward.

Sarah nipped at my jaw. "This is why we do it," she growled. "We want to be close. We want to touch them." She squeezed her hand. I flinched and made a noise in my throat. "We want, don't we? We always want. More and more. I know you are weak. I know you can't help yourself. You want her, don't you? You've always wanted her."

"Jesus, Sarah, I—"

Lolita sat down at a table in the back of the room. There were other people with her, people I didn't recognize.

Sarah's hand withdrew from my pants. "Show me." Her voice was right in my ear, her words slipping into my brain. "Show me how much you want her. Go over and tell her. Tell her the truth."

"Tell her what? I'm not—"

A man and a woman bounced off the dance floor. She stumbled. He caught her. They bumped into us, laughing at their clumsiness. He had an expensive smile. She was wearing a diamond necklace. Apologies were traded, and they rolled into the hall that led to the bathrooms. I fumbled with my pants.

Sarah was . . . Sarah was gone.

I looked around wildly. If she was on the dance floor, who knew how long it would take me to find her in that press of bodies. Down the hall? I couldn't remember if anyone else had gone that way with the laughing pair.

My belt was undone, as were several of the buttons on my jeans. I tidied up. When I raised my head, I noticed Lolita Brigade was looking right at me. I did that thing you always see in the movies where the nerdy guy looks around to check if there is a hunky guy standing behind him. I caught myself as I was doing it, which made my entire reaction even dumber.

At least, I didn't point at myself and raise my eyebrows like I couldn't believe she was looking at me.

I did, however, take two steps toward her.

And that was when the fire alarm went off, and the place became a madhouse.

The floor became a flood of bodies and I let myself be carried by their surge. Outside, the alley was no less packed. People were trying to get out to Sunset. People were coming in from the road. I was jostled and tossed about like a piece of trash until I managed to dart out to the sidewalk.

Police cars and fire trucks were filling Sunset, painting the night with their flashing lights. Cops shouted at people to move away from the building. I ducked my head and followed directions. A uniform waved me toward the end of the block, and when I reached the intersection, I kept on going. Head down. Hands in pockets. Walk anyway and keep walking. Put the lights and excitement behind you.

I hadn't smelled smoke and I hadn't seen fire. Someone must have pulled the fire alarm on accident. Maybe one of the pair who had bumbled into Sarah and me. Maybe Sarah had done it as part of whatever weird high she had been on. It didn't matter. I didn't need to be there anymore. My chest was tight, and my blood was racing through my veins.

Sarah's questions pinged around my head. Did I want her? Was I—like all the other guys at Burko's—obsessed with Lolita? I flashed on the life-sized poster. On the shape of her body beneath that tight t-shirt. On the way the camera lingered on her as she ran across the sand. Is that what I wanted?

I focused on more tangible things: Sarah's hands on me. The taste of her mouth. Her body pressed against me. The three thousand, eight hundred, and who the fuck cares how many days it had been since I had had warm human contact.

By the time Huggy found me, several miles closer to the water, I had convinced myself that I didn't want anything. I went along with Huggy because I was free. I let Sarah lead because I was without ego. I was a leaf, floating on the wind. A stone, rolling down a hill. I wasn't responsible. Forces greater than myself were carrying me.

The story broke two days later: Lolita Brigade was missing. Last time anyone had seen her had been at The Wink, an exclusive club on Sunset. Right before someone pulled the fire alarm and caused a panic.

We gathered at Bernard's place. The cast posters had come down, except for Lolita's. Bernard had filled the wall around her with printouts from news outlets and hand-drawn maps. The other roommate—Allen—was making a collage out of paparazzi photos gleaned from someone's personal collection of magazine clippings. Gina sat a folding table, color-coding lines on several sheets of paper. She was wearing a stylish pair of jeans and layered t-shirts—a much hipper look than she had sported the other night. She even had her hair tastefully in control. A lock dangled against her neck. It was a nice touch.

She caught me looking. "What?"

"It's a good-looking system," I said.

People reacted to drama in all sorts of ways.

"Where are Trevor and Randy?" Burko asked. He had run out of paper to tape to the wall.

"Trevor's working. Randy had tickets to the Dodgers game," Gina said.

Burko's expression said he didn't care for Randy's priorities.

"Flip said he'd be here in an hour or two," Allen offered.

Christi was sitting cross-legged on one of the sofas, staring at her laptop screen.

"Where is—" My question died under a stern glance from Huggy.

He cleared his throat. "What do we know?" he asked.

"Not a goddamned—" Burko started, but Gina spoke over him.

"The local NBC affiliate said she didn't show up for her call time yesterday. One of the gossip sites is claiming a reliable source says the producers covered for her. The crew shot B-roll stuff and pick-ups so the production wouldn't lose the entire day. When she didn't show this morning, the director and the showrunner called the studio. The studio scrambled and sent people to all the places she hangs out. The crew sat around until lunch, at which time, the talent was sent home and the set was shut down for the day. That's when the news broke wide."

"Okay," Huggy said. "That's a start."

Burko put up his hand. "Hang on, Hugh. Who put you in charge?"

Huggy looked at him and spread his hands.

"This is my Ops Center," Burko said without a trace of irony in his voice.

"Yeah, so?"

Burko gestured at the poster of Lolita. "She's my—" He stopped before he embarrassed himself. "It's my room," he said, falling back to safer ground.

"Who took those continuing education classes at Shoreline Community College? The criminology ones?" Huggy asked.

Burko bit his lip. Everyone's expression said they knew the answers to Huggy's questions.

"And who has written an actual screenplay?" Huggy asked, really working to make his point. "About cops, I might add. A heavily-researched screenplay."

Gina cleared her throat.

"What?" Huggy asked.

"Maybe . . ." she started.

"Maybe what?"

"Maybe you're . . . maybe you're too close to this," she said.

"What do you mean by that?"

She fiddled with the errant lock of hair. "I'm just—I mean, I'm not saying—it's just maybe you're . . ."

Huggy's gaze dared her to finish.

"Maybe you're a little too fixated on the person we're looking for," I said, stepping in for Gina.

He whirled on me. "What the fuck does that mean?"

"You said it yourself," I said. "Someone was stalking her."

That got everyone's attention. Huggy held up his hands to hold off their questions. "What are you talking about?"

"Remember when you picked me up in the Valley?" I said. "After I had been thrown off the studio lot? We talked about the stupid shit people do around celebrities. Well, you talked about it. You thought I was obsessed with some movie star and that I had tried to sneak into her trailer or something. I said it wasn't anything like that, and I pointed out that it was kind of pot-and-kettle for you to be calling me out like that when . . ."

"When what?" There was an edge to Huggy's tone.

I paused, thinking about how I was going to proceed. Gina caught my eye and gave me a raised eyebrow, letting me know she had my back, which was a nice gesture.

Galvanized by the courtesy of a near-stranger, I continued. "You and I had met a few days before that. When *Beach Patrol* was shooting at the Ralphs in Westwood. We got chased off, remember? You told me all about her: how no one saw her true talent; that what her career needed was a breakout movie—something with a really good script that showcased all her talents. A script about cops, I guess."

"Oh, for fuck's sake," Gina said.

Huggy flushed. "It's a good script," he snapped.

"Is that the script you've been working on?" Burko asked. "Something for *her*?"

"What? And you haven't been?" Huggy shot back. "At least mine is a big screen vehicle. Not like your Skinemax wank-fest."

"It's an anthology project," Burko said archly. "It's meant to showcase—"

"Uh, guys?" Christi broke up the screenwriter slap fest. She had turned her laptop so we could see the screen. "I think we have a problem."

It was an online gossip site. The headline read: *Ex-Con Celebrity Stalker.* The picture accompanying the article was a booking photo, taken—well, three thousand, eight hundred and who the fuck cares days ago.

Everyone looked at the photo and then looked at me and then looked at the photo again. It was a classic bit of scene blocking for the cheap seats in the back of the auditorium.

"Huh," I said, keeping my voice as casual as possible. "Not my best photo."

Mentally, I was scrambling to figure out the best way to tell them without telling them, but Christi—who had no trouble reading upside-down—beat me to it. "Holy shit, you did porn?"

Another round of double takes, followed by a bunch of questions that had nothing to do with why we were in Burko's rec room. What kind of porn? How long? Had I had violated indecency laws? Did California have indecency laws? Who was the hottest girl I slept with? Had I been violated in—

"It was for cocaine," I said, cutting off the questions before they got out of hand.

"How long?" Gina asked again.

I gave her a *Are you asking about length of time or something else?* look, and she blushed when she realized there was more than one answer to her question.

"Ten years," I said, providing the socially-appropriate answer. "I got out a few weeks ago. Huggy was"—I gestured at him—"*is* the first friend I've had in a decade."

"What?" Huggy looked stunned.

"Yeah. Look, it's hard to meet people in prison," I said. "A lot of them don't stick around and—"

"We're friends?"

I stared at him. "I've been sleeping on your sofa for a week. We binge-watched three seasons of *Beach Patrol* together."

"Whoa," Allen said, his first contribution to the conversation in the last few minutes.

Huggy and I looked at him. He put up his shoulders and

mumbled when he spoke. "Burko won't let me watch his tapes," he said.

"They're SLP," Burko said. "You have to be very careful when you rewind them."

Huggy screwed up his face. "SLP? You put them on SLP?"

Burko made a fist. "It's more economical that way," he said. "It uses fewer tapes."

"Yeah, but the quality is for—"

"Boys," Gina said, interrupting the home video nerd talk. "This male bonding is fun to watch, but can we get back to the important stuff?"

Christi smirked. "Yeah," she said. "Like 'How long?'"

Gina slapped the table. "That's not—"

"Long enough," interrupted a new voice.

Sarah stood in the doorway to the rest of the house. Her hair was a mess and she looked like she had been beaten with a sack of cats and then thrown out of a car. Certain she had all of our attention, she said, very dramatically: "It's Phil."

And then she collapsed.

*You have to compress the narrative in a script,* Huggy told me during our binge on *Beach Patrol. You only have forty-two minutes to tell a story. You don't have time to go into all the details, and your audience knows this. They've sat through two acts already. They've been watching the show for a year. They don't care about the facts. They know what happens next. You don't have to convince them.*

I had wanted to argue with him, but then I had thought about my trial. By the time the DA was finished with his case, we were done. Everyone had sat through two acts already. They didn't care about the facts. They were there to see justice happen. They were there to see the good guys win.

Sarah had that in common with the LA District Attorney: *know your audience.*

We didn't care about facts. We were eager for the chase scene in the third act. We were eager to be the good guys.

The self-storage lot was in West LA. It had a high fence, and the gate was locked. There was a keypad entry system. "What's the code?" Huggy asked as he pulled up next to the pad.

"How the fuck should I know?"

"Didn't she tell us the code?"

Sarah said a lot of things when she woke up: garbled half-sentences, some song lyrics, a bit that sounded like dialogue from last week's episode, and Phil's name. Over and over. Burko had finally yelled for all of us to leave the room so he could get her calm. We had acquiesced, but Huggy lasted less than a minute before creeping back into the living room, where we had taken Sarah after she had passed out. A little bit later, he had flagged me down. *I know where he's got her*, he had said.

Phil had watched the same show we had. He knew better than to take his victims back to his place. *He's got a storage unit*, Huggy said as we sped across LA. *They always have a storage unit.*

"Sarah told *you* about this place," I said to Huggy, reminding him of how we had gotten here.

Huggy slapped the steering wheel. "Fuck," he exclaimed. He glared at the fence. "How are we supposed to get in there without a code?"

The fence was topped with a single strand of barbed wire, which—to me—was like tying a shoestring across a gap in a pasture fence and telling the cows to stay put. "The usual way," I said. I let out a small laugh.

"Oh, man," Huggy whined. "What if there's a dog?"

I got out of the car and approached the fence. There were three rows of storage units, and each unit had an outside facing door that rolled up. I starting whistling as I walked along the fence, keeping an eye out for black shadows with lots of teeth. I got to the end of the lot without seeing anything.

In fact . . .

I turned and hurried back to Huggy's Jeep. "Where's his car?" I asked. I waved a hand at the empty aisles between the rows. "If Phil was here, his car would be parked outside one of these units, wouldn't it?"

Huggy scratched his chin. "Unless he parked it a block away or something," he said.

"And what? Hauled Lolita back here in a sack?"

He shrugged. "Maybe he stashed her and then moved his car."

I shook my head. "That's a lot of work," I said. "Besides, that's too many details."

He didn't follow.

"It's something you said about scripts," I said. "When we were watching that episode about the twins who—it doesn't matter."

"Wait. Are you talking about the episode with the twins who killed their step-dad and stuffed him in—"

"It's not important," I interrupted.

"You think he's cut her up already?" Huggy was still stuck on the *Beach Patrol* episode.

"No, that's not what I'm talking about."

"Oh, man. That's some sick shit." Huggy's hands tightened on the steering wheel. "If he—if he—"

"Details," I said sharply. "Too many details make things too complicated. That's what you told me. We don't care about all the complicated bits. All we want is to get to the end."

He frowned. "This isn't the end?"

"Phil isn't going to drive in here, stash Lolita in his secret stash spot or whatever it is, and then go move his car. That's too complicated. That's not what he's thinking. He's thinking—"

"Sex dungeon," Huggy said. "He's thinking 'sex dungeon.'"

"No, that's not what I meant, but, okay, maybe that's—" I hesitated, a bit of memory tugging at me. I fumbled for it, like I was trying to grab a fluttering slip of paper.

I almost had it when I heard the sirens.

"No way," Huggy breathed. He stared at me. "Do you think—?"

I yanked the door open and hopped into the car. "Get us out of here," I said. Huggy fumbled with the gear selector, found reverse, and jerked us into the street. I popped the passenger side seat back so I was out of sight. The sirens got louder, and the cab of the Jeep filled with flashing red and blue lights. Huggy fluttered the gas pedal. I held my breath.

The siren wailed loudly and then started to fade. The lights went with it, and the inside of the Jeep filled with shadows.

He drove without speaking. Both hands on the wheel. Eyes locked on the road.

I exhaled.

"I think we're clear," he said. He put his foot on the brake and the Jeep eased to a stop. A steady red glow illuminated his face. We were at a traffic light.

I had been thinking frantically, trying not to get caught up in what could have happened if the cops had found us at the self-storage place. "Phil's," I said. "They're at Phil's."

"Are you sure?"

"No," I admitted. "But the same rules apply, don't they?"

"What rules?"

"Keep it simple. Plus . . ."

"Plus what?"

"'Sex dungeon,'" I said.

Huggy remembered what Phil had said. "He didn't deny it," he said. "When Sarah brought it up the other night. He started to say something, but he caught himself."

I nodded. "You know where Phil lives, don't you?"

Huggy flushed. "What. No. I mean—" He ducked his head and looked up at the traffic light. He mumbled something that might have been a confession.

I didn't care how or why he knew. In fact, I would have been more surprised if he hadn't. Huggy liked knowing more than he should about things.

☆

Huggy pointed out the building as we drove past. There was a self-service copy center and a donut shop on the first floor. Three or four apartments filled the second floor. We found the alley, and Huggy turned off the Jeep's headlights as we eased toward a parking area in the back. Huggy pointed at a worn-out Subaru parked close to the building. "That's Phil's," he said.

"See?" I said. "Close by. Not blocks away."

Huggy parked on the Subaru's bumper and we approached the building. The back door had a window in it, and inside, we saw a staircase leading up to the apartments. The door was locked, and Huggy pulled metal strips from his wallet and worked them into the keyhole. I nonchalantly looked around for security cameras, late night watchers, and attack dogs. I didn't see any of those things, and told Huggy we were clear. "You can stop fussing with that thing," I said.

"I'm not fussing with it," he said. "It's a little . . ."

I looked around again. He was taking a really long time. "Maybe we should break the glass . . ." I suggested.

"I got this," he snapped.

"Didn't you take a community college class?"

"They don't teach lock-picking at community college." His face lit up. "Aha," he said.

The doorknob turned when he tried it.

"See?" he said. "Piece of cake."

Inside the building, a hall led to the street entrance. In the foyer, a rack of mailboxes was attached to the wall. The nameplates had first initials and last names. One of them was "P. Chase."

"Number three," I said to Huggy as we went up the stairs. There were only four doors upstairs, so it wasn't hard to figure out which one was Phil's.

Huggy had his lock picks ready, but I stopped him before he started fumbling with the lock. "Try it," I said.

"Why? No one leaves their door unlocked."

I tried the knob. It turned in my hand. "Shit," I said. I took a step back.

"What?" Huggy reached for the door.

"Don't." I stopped him before he could push it open. "What if you're right?"

"Right about what?"

"If no one leaves their door unlocked, why is this one unlocked?"

"You're the one who thought it might be unlocked!"

"Yeah, I did, but I didn't—shit."

Light from a passing car's headlights lit up the window at the end of the hall. Huggy and I both flinched. We froze like stunned rabbits, our bodies straining to hear or see or sense something. The window darkened. The only sounds were Huggy's breathing and the echo of my heart thumping in my chest.

"What's going on, Bliss?" Huggy was whispering now.

"I don't know," I said. "I'm just thinking. What if . . . shit . . . what if we're supposed to find the door unlocked?"

"Okay. What if?"

"Back at the storage place. Were the cops coming to catch us or were they going somewhere else?"

"I dunno, Bliss. We got the fuck out of there."

"Sarah told us about the storage unit. She didn't tell us about Phil's place."

"So, we should have scaled the fence?"

"No, that's not it." I shook my head "Phil's car is downstairs. He's not at the storage unit."

Huggy gestured with his hands. "What the fuck are you talking about?"

I pointed at the doorknob. "Why is that door unlocked?"

"I don't fucking know, Bliss!" His voice was louder. "Why don't we open the fucking door and find out?"

"No, wait—"

But he was done listening. He grabbed the doorknob and opened the door. I tensed, not sure what was going to happen but half-expecting something.

From somewhere inside Phil's apartment, a woman spoke. "For fuck's sake, would you two idiots untie me already?"

Burko yelped with surprise when he spotted me in the doorway to the Ops Center. "Jesus Christ," he said. "You scared the shit out of me."

"That's what everyone says when they see him," I said.

The *Beach Patrol* gang rushed me like I was a minor celebrity, and the room was filled with their eager questions. I put up my hands to ward them off. "She was at Phil's," I said. "Huggy volunteered to stay with her until—"

"Of course he did." Burko made no effort to hide his bitterness.

"And Phil?" Allen asked.

"He wasn't home," I said, which was the truth.

"So he was the kidnapper?"

I wasn't sure how to answer that question, so I shrugged.

Gina asked the important question: "What about the storage unit? Sarah gave you the address to a storage unit. Why did you go to Phil's?"

"You know, that's a very good question. In fact, I'd like to ask Sarah about that. Where is she?"

Burko frowned. "Didn't you—?" He gestured toward the front of the house. "She's out there. On the couch. Right where—"

"We wanted to take her to the hospital," Allen said. "But she said she wanted the police to see her like she was."

"And which of you called the police?" I asked.

Allen looked at Burko. "I thought . . ." He started.

Burko looked at Gina. "That was . . ."

Gina looked at Christi, and they both shared similar *Men are such morons* looks.

I sighed and asked a less awkward question: "Is there beer in the fridge?"

Burko nodded absently.

I went to the kitchen, found a beer in the refrigerator, opened it, and wandered into the dark living room. I sat down on the empty sofa and sipped my beer. It was cold. So was the couch.

*She was engaged to Hutton Chandler,* Huggy had told me during the drive to Phil's. *But Chandler was a method actor, and when his character—Ricky Boston—got obsessed about Lolita, I mean Dierdra, so did Chandler. The writers didn't warn him about getting his character getting killed. And, well, he kinda freaked out when it happened.*

*Kinda?*

Huggy shook his head. *Yeah, it was weird. And awkward. I mean, the tabloids ate it up, and, look, it wrecked their relationship. Chandler's and Sarah's. And she blamed Lolita.*

*The others know?*

He thought about that for a while. *Gina,* he said. *Maybe Christi.*

*And Phil?*

Huggy hadn't been sure, and, well, no one could ask Phil. I had found his body in the dumpster behind the building when I was leaving.

It had been a hunch that had made me stop and check. That special radar learned during a decade of incarceration. You learned how to read those stillnesses that weren't natural.

After we had untied Lolita, Huggy had shooed me off. *Take my car and go back to Bernard's,* he said. *I got this.*

We were in Phil's living room, next to the chair where Lolita had been tied. She was in the kitchen, talking to her manager on the phone. It had been a strange moment, like we had been on the cusp of something.

As soon as she hung up, her manager would call Beach Patrol's producers, who would, in turn, call other people. Fixers. PR managers. Other executives. Eventually, the world would find out that Lolita Brigade had been found, but before that, everyone was going to figure out the story they were going to tell.

Huggy knew this moment wasn't going to last. *This is my chance,* he had whispered as he shoved me toward the door. *I gotta pitch my script. I gotta tell her my story.*

There's always that moment, isn't there? When you pause and talk directly to the audience. *See, this is how it happened.* You don't want to bog it down with *all* the details, but some of them are necessary. You've got to tie it all together. You share enough so that they can make the jump with you.

See, this is how it happened: Sarah had known Lolita was going to be at the club that night. All that sexy talk and grab-by-grabby had been wind me up. To push me toward Lolita. It didn't matter if I had made contact. I was there. That was all she needed. I was the ex-con in the room when the Hollywood star disappeared. I was exactly the sort of salacious tip a less-than-reputable gossip site would eagerly snap up.

Sarah had pulled the fire alarm, and during the ensuing confusion, she had convinced Lolita she was supposed to take care of her. She was working for the producers. Extra security they had hired. Whatever. *The details don't matter.* Lolita had believed her.

Earlier that night, Phil had joked about letting Lolita cuff him. It probably wasn't the first time he had said something crass like that, and over the next few days, the rest of the gang at Bernard's would recall other comments on other nights—all of which would color the picture being drawn by the media. Portrait of an Obsessed Fan. And that was how this episode was going to break down: Hollywood star, obsessed fan, hint of a sex dungeons, body in the dumpster. Not exactly ratings gold, but every season has those run-of-the-mill episodes that stick close to the show bible.

Why mess with what works?

Other than a bump on the head and some rope burns, Lolita hadn't been hurt. Which meant that Sarah—who definitely looked like she had gone several rounds—had fought with someone else. I was a little surprised that Phil had had the opportunity. Sarah struck me as the type who would smack you with a rock when you weren't looking.

I sipped my beer. It was a cold kiss against my lips.

I appreciated sitting on a busted sofa and sipping a beer. There wasn't beer in prison. Furniture was worse there, too.

I wondered what it was like to kill a man. I wondered how long it would take her to realize that was going to shadow her for the rest of her life. She would never be rid of it.

I sipped my beer again.

Freedom had a nice taste to it.

✳

## Get Harry

Building a relationship with my readers is one of the marvelous parts of being a writer, and the best way that relationship grows is through interaction. The only way I know these stories are making you laugh, cry, or shake your fist in joy is by hearing from you. The easiest way you can let me know that you'd like to see more stories of this crew is to leave a review.

Reviews don't have to be complicated. All you need is a place to leave a few words about the book (the retailer where you purchased this book, an online review site, or—heck!—even a hand-drawn sign works). Let me know what you think about Barton and Blake and Hecate and Butch. Be discrete about the Discrete Detective though. He prefers that.

Also, the Harry Bryant mailing list is very low-traffic. It's the best way to stay informed, and signing up lets me know that you're a fan and you'd like to see more.

http://www.harrybryantwriter.com/mailinglist.php

Thanks for your support!

Harry Bryant lives in the Pacific Northwest with a house full of pretty books.

Find him on the web at http://www.harrybryantwriter.com